# Fairy Tales and War Stories

J. Thomas Hennessey, Jr. PhD

# Table of Contents

# Overview and Introduction

I was once asked what the difference was between a fairy tale and a war story because, to this person, there seemed to be some similarity. I responded that I believed the difference was that a fairy tale started with the phrase "Once upon a time." On the other hand, a war story started with the phrase, "Now, this is no bullshit."

The collection of stories contained herein is a compilation of "fairy tales and war stories." While they span fifty years, they are from two entirely different cultures. The first is the more than twenty years spent in the US Army, and the other is the twenty years spent in higher education. While the reader may find similarities between the two cultures, I continue to marvel at the major differences I experienced. Each has been selected because it includes something interesting that I experienced, and after telling these "fairy tales and war stories," I was encouraged to write them down and share them with others.

While each of these stories could be a personal experience, they almost always involve others. I have tried to treat them all with dignity and respect. I beg the reader's indulgence for referencing so many senior officials, but it is something that the Army and higher education offer that few other occupations can.

Chapters 1-20 cover the Army career from Second Lieutenant to Colonel. The events experienced include service in Vietnam, two tours on the Joint Chiefs of Staff, and United States Army Attaché to the Court of St James, American Embassy, London, UK. Chapters 21-34 cover some unique experiences in higher education that I had after joining George Mason University.

# Chapter 1: A Butter Bar Lieutenant

As an Army brat, I only knew the US Army from a specific perspective, living on an Army Post and surrounded by soldiers. However, my first assignments after ROTC commissioning differed: one at the Infantry Center and School at Ft. Benning, Georgia, and another at Ft. Ord, California, for assignment as a basic training officer.

Duty as a "training officer" was not particularly difficult. However, extra duties and details made balancing requirements and deadlines essential learning experiences. Two of those learning experiences occurred when I was assigned the additional duty of company mess officer and battalion duty officer. As the mess officer, I was responsible for the operation of the mess hall and feeding the 240 trainees. I learned that the mess sergeant was taking a full ration of coffee when the trainees would barely drink coffee. After additional investigation, we successfully court-martialed the sergeant for misappropriation of government property and black marketeering. He had been selling the coffee and other mess hall equipment at a local flea market.

The battalion duty officer was an additional detail that every officer was required to perform monthly. Among other requirements, we randomly checked the barracks before and after midnight to ensure proper ventilation procedures were followed. At this time, Ft. Ord was at the height of the concern for upper respiratory infections among trainees. As a precaution, the duty officer was responsible for ensuring maximum ventilation throughout the barracks. The final responsibility of the duty officer for that day was to take the report from a designated company at its first formation at 0600. This meant that I had to be in place at 0600 when a First Sergeant took the platoon reports and then turned and reported to either the company commander or, in my case, the battalion duty officer.

Unfortunately, I didn't wake up until 0545 that morning. I sped to the battalion area just in enough time to walk through the door as the first sergeant of A Company was turning around to give his report. I believe this "significant emotional event" more than any other developed an instinct to wake up when I needed to, rather than waiting to be awakened. That served me well later in Vietnam. One of my

more memorable assignments as a new Lieutenant was organizing the Brigade function at the Officers Club on the beach. It was an enormous building on the beach, and the team assigned to prepare for the planned "Monte Carlo" night did an outstanding job. Unfortunately, I only remember a little of the evening. Still, I remember getting a letter of appreciation from the Brigade commander for the event's success. Such is the life of a "butter bar." One of our favorite events at Ft Ord

was the spring social. This picture shows us in our finery at the Officers' Club.

# Chapter 2: The First Year in Vietnam

The trip to Saigon in 1966 was not a memorable one. I remember a long flight from San Francisco and arriving at Saigon airport in mid-morning. The actual arrival was another matter. The sights and smells are something one always remembers. The heat was like a giant, wet washcloth draped over your head. The smells were indescribable, and only later were you able to sort out the various components: charcoal, diesel fuel, rancid fish sauce, and human excrement. It is a cocktail that defies description. After several days of orientations on in-country activities at the Replacement depot in Saigon, I was on a C-130 aircraft to Pleiku in the central highlands and the 3rd Brigade, 25th Infantry Division. I reported to the Brigade replacement detachment because only the 3rd Brigade was in Pleiku, while the Division headquarters and the other two brigades were in Cu Chi.

The 3rd Brigade had deployed to Vietnam the previous December and was operating in the Central Highlands. I was assigned to the 2d Battalion, 35th Infantry (Cacti Blue), commanded by LTC Phillip R. Feir, and then on to Charlie Company. Charlie Company was in the 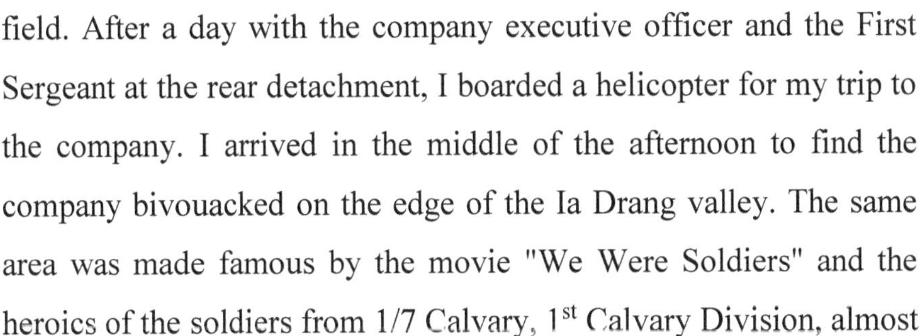 field. After a day with the company executive officer and the First Sergeant at the rear detachment, I boarded a helicopter for my trip to the company. I arrived in the middle of the afternoon to find the company bivouacked on the edge of the Ia Drang valley. The same area was made famous by the movie "We Were Soldiers" and the heroics of the soldiers from 1/7 Calvary, 1st Calvary Division, almost a year earlier. In fact, the 3rd Brigade, 25th Infantry Division, at that time, was commanded by Colonel Hal Moore, who had commanded the 1/7 Cavalry a year earlier. I replaced a lieutenant who was wounded the week before in an on-again-off-again encounter with units from the North Vietnamese Army (NVA), sometimes called the second battle of the Ia Drang.

I spent the better part of the afternoon that first day in the field, being introduced to my squad leaders and learning more about the platoon from the platoon sergeant. The 25th Division had been stationed in Hawaii since the end of World War II. Not surprisingly, most of the noncommissioned officers in the company were Hawaiian. My four squad leaders, two Sergeant E5s and two Staff Sergeant E6s, were related by blood or marriage to the Platoon Sergeant, E7. Late that afternoon, the company commander called all the platoon leaders and issued an operations order for the next day's operation. We were going to make a combat assault (CA) into a landing zone (LZ) in the Ia Drang that would then be followed by a company search and destroy operation against NVA units that were reported to be operating in the area. My platoon would be the third platoon into the LZ.

I then met with my platoon sergeant and squad leaders, and we worked out the sequence of loads for the platoon the next morning. Hardly able to sleep that night, I was up early, and after some coffee and C ration ham and eggs, we began to form up for the helicopters. Depending upon the size of the landing zone, each slick (troop carrier) carried eight soldiers. For this CA, our lift LZ was more than

a football field long.
Five groups of four
soldiers were on each
side of the long LZ.
This meant that each
lift would have five

ships landing one behind the other, and the soldiers would load from

each side of the aircraft. A check of equipment was standard

operating procedure, and squad leaders checked each soldier to

ensure they had all the necessary weapons, ammunition, food, and

water. Although I had a couple of opportunities to ride in helicopters

while at Ft. Benning, the arrival of five UH-1s, their quick loading,

and then taking off was a memorable first experience. That first ride

was amazing. You could see the mountains, the valleys, the streams,

and everything so green it almost hurt your eyes. It did not seem like

a long ride because, before I knew it, we were following the other

helicopters into the landing zone.

I will never forget the first sight of artillery explosions on the

edges of the LZ, gunships firing rockets into the LZ. Our choppers

flew in fast, disgorging soldiers in seconds and then quickly pulling

pitch to get out. As we approached the LZ, I tried to remember what I

had learned about air assault operations and found myself pitifully ill-

prepared. Because the choppers were coming into the LZ so fast, they

would flair to slow their forward speed and then settle to the ground.

As we got closer, green tracers of the North Vietnamese Army began to lift toward our formation. Immediately to my left, the door gunner began to fire long bursts from his M60 pedestal-mounted machine gun. As the hot ammunition casings from the M60 hit my helmet and slid down my back, my RTO (radiotelephone operator) nudged me. I assumed that the flair of the aircraft meant that we had landed, so I jumped out the door of the chopper. To my surprise, we were still some 15-20 feet off the ground. Fortunately, the ground was quite muddy. I sank to my ankles so that when they got off the chopper, my RTO and the platoon medic pulled me up and said, "Let's go, Lieutenant." The platoon was somewhat suspicious of me for weeks after that episode. Some said later that they weren't sure if I was another "John Wayne" or just stupid. Either way, I was dangerous.

A steep learning curve is the best description of my first couple of months as a platoon leader in combat. Although we were almost constantly in the field, contact with the enemy was generally sporadic. My land navigation skills, ability to adjust artillery fire, and patrolling improved considerably during these first weeks and months.

Among the inevitable humorous events in a combat zone was while out on a platoon patrol, I was called to the point location by one of my squad leaders. The point man was a soldier everyone called "Cherry Boy." Cherry Boy was standing on one leg and as motionless as I have seen a one-legged soldier. The squad leader pointed to the ground around Cherry Boy and traced the outline of one huge snake. When we located its head, I whispered to Cherry Boy that he should jump to the side as soon as I pulled the trigger on my shotgun. I aimed at the head and fired. I have never seen anyone jump so high and so far on one leg. We pulled out the snake to find that it was a King Cobra approximately nine feet long. When you stretched out its hood, it covered your chest.

I received my Combat Infantry Badge in October 1965, confirming my more than 60 days in combat operations. In late November 1966, the NVA attacked the Special Forces camp at Plei Djrang, and 2/35 was tasked to respond. C Company was assigned as the lead element. My platoon was loaded aboard tanks hustling along trails and roads to get to the SF camp as quickly as possible. As we approached the Special Forces compound, the lead tank I was riding on hit an improvised explosive device (IED) comprised of a 250 lb. bomb that effectively immobilized the tank and wounded five of us on the tank. The explosion deafened me, hit me with fragments, and I was eventually medically evacuated to the 7th Field Hospital in Nha Trang. While I was in the hospital, C Company and A Company experienced some of the most brutal fighting of the year.

Upon my return to the unit, I was informed by the Battalion Executive Officer that I was going to be the Battalion S4 or logistics officer. I learned later that the S4, a Captain, had been medically evacuated and that LTC Feir had personally selected the replacement. Although I cannot confirm it, I suspect that LTC Feir used the after-action reports that each Lieutenant was required to write after an enemy engagement as the basis for his decision. Like my counterparts, mine came back from the battalion commander with multiple red marks. We learned that LTC Feir had been the English department chair at West Point and insisted that his officers knew how to communicate. That meant that his officers must be able to document what they had experienced in combat in writing appropriately. My reports were impressive or at least caught his attention.

The tour as S4 was as frustrating as it was educational. First, I had just been promoted to First Lieutenant and was the most junior officer on the battalion staff. Second, I was the only primary staff officer at our base camp in Pleiku, and I was charged with ensuring that the troops in the field had everything they needed to survive and succeed. That responsibility alone often put me at odds with the four company executive officers of the line companies who were always trying to get all they could for the soldiers of their individual companies. Finally, I was also responsible for the final construction of our battalion facilities. These facilities included renovated barracks for the troops and a motor pool for the vehicles. My days were long, and had it not been for the Chief Warrant Officer 3 (CW3) property book officer, I would have made it through the first week.

Not long after the change of command for LTC Feir, I pestered the new battalion commander, LTC Clinton Grainger, to let me return to the field as a platoon leader. He finally relented, and I took command of 1st Platoon, A Company, with CPT Luis C. Barcena as the company commander. CPT Barcena was a short, pugnacious Cuban who had survived the Bay of Pigs and was commissioned a captain for his service to the US. Hard-charging but unfamiliar with the terrain and operations in the Central Highlands, CPT Barcena often pushed us harder than we thought possible. He was not easy to get along with in the field. During one company-sized operation, he regularly relieved one point platoon leader after the other because he thought none of us knew how to navigate well enough. One day alone, my platoon rotated through the point at least three times before we led everyone back to the battalion base camp late one night. To make things even more frustrating, the more agitated CPT Barcena became, the less we could understand him on the radio as his English deteriorated in direct proportion to his agitation.

One of the more surreal events during that year did not involve a firefight but rather the discovery of a downed aircraft from a year before. During a platoon patrol, one of my squads entered a thick group of trees and immediately notified me that they had found an aircraft. The A1E Skyraider aircraft was almost upside down with its tail in the air and perfectly hidden from the air and ground. You literally had to be next to it to see it. We discovered the pilot's remains and all the onboard weapons and ammunition. We called it in and secured the area until it was lifted out by a heavy recovery helicopter. There was one bullet hole in the canopy, and it had apparently struck and killed the pilot. We learned later that it was actually one of the aircraft that had supported the 1st Cavalry the year before, during the first battle of the Ia Drang. Recalling what had happened a year ago on this battlefield made it a lonely wait in a totally exposed position and surreal beyond anything I had yet experienced. I remember looking at the Chu Pong mountains about five kilometers away and recognizing that an entire NVA division has been in those mountains attempting to take out 1/7th Cavalry the year before.

After four more months in the field and multiple enemy engagements, LTC Grainger asked me to return to the battalion staff as the S1 or adjutant. As the adjutant, I was responsible for the Battalion's personnel and administrative functions. Among these was the processing of recommendations for awards. One, in particular, was important to me, and I took responsibility for preparing the entire packet for Steve Karopczyc's Medal of Honor recommendation. Almost a year after the actions of October 1966, 1LT Stephen Karopczyc was posthumously awarded the Medal of Honor, one of three awarded to soldiers of the 2/35 Infantry during the Vietnam War. I also received my second Purple Heart as the battalion adjutant. Our base camp was attacked one evening by enemy sappers who had infiltrated the wire perimeter guarded by a Marine company and threw satchel TNT charges into our bunkers and tents. I managed to get out of my bunker while a VC was shooting into it. I dove into a nearby ditch and exchanged gunfire with him. I'm unsure if I hit him or if he ran out of ammo and left. Fortunately, I received only minor fragmentation wounds from the grenade he threw after me in the ditch. Unfortunately, a satchel charge killed one of my clerks in the S1 section, which also killed the VC sapper that put it in the S1 tent. We kept the battalion plaques given to all departing officers in that same tent. Mine has a few dents from the shrapnel caused by the satchel charge that night.

I left Vietnam in August 1967, a very different lieutenant than the one that had arrived the year before. My arrival at Seattle-Tacoma (SEATAC) airport was uneventful as the demonstrations and anti-war rhetoric had yet to peak. However, on the plane ride to Louisville, Kentucky, that stopped in three other airports, I was told by a stewardess that since three other soldiers and I were traveling on Army-issued "space available tickets," we might be "bumped" by college students heading back to school. I told her that the four of us had been in the jungle for a year, and it would probably take more than the crew of that aircraft to get us off before our scheduled stop. Shortly after we took off from SEATAC, the pilot returned to me and said I should not worry. All four of us would be on the plane until we reached our destinations.

I leave it to the reader to decide how much of this was a "fairy tale" and how much a "war story."

# Chapter 3: Fort Leonard Wood and McNamara's 100,000

Upon my return from Vietnam in 1967, I received a thirty-day leave. After visiting family, we headed to a new assignment at Ft Leonard Wood, Missouri. Affectionately referred to as Fort Lost in the Woods as it was so far from any recognizable town. Assigned to the 1st Battalion of the 2nd Basic Combat Training Brigade (BCT), I reported to the unit. I cannot remember the name of the battalion commander, but I do remember his first question to me as I stood in his office. "Hennessey, was your old man ever the IG (Inspector General) of the 82nd Airborne?" My affirmative reply elicited the comment, "Hennessey, I don't think we will get along." I never found out why his experience with my father was a negative one, but I can only assume it affected him significantly,

As a promotable First Lieutenant, I was assigned to command C Company, 1st Battalion, 2nd Basic Combat Training Brigade. The company had an experienced mix of Drill Instructors (DIs). Some seasoned old-timers knew their jobs and did them well. Some young Vietnam vets thought they knew everything. And some young DIs really didn't care much about what they did. Pulling this diverse crew together was challenging and often frustrating.

The First Sergeant was the epitome of a great soldier. Ever the professional, he guided me in ways I only now realize. I will always remember his coffee, a strong brew ready each morning, regardless of how early I might arrive. Before turning the pot on, he put a little salt and some clean eggshells in the coffee grounds. To this day, I put a little sugar in my coffee to offset the small bit of salt I experienced in his coffee. I was sorry to see him retire about halfway through my command tour. My promotion to Captain, while expected, nonetheless gave me the feeling that I had made the right career decision.

Basic training had evolved since my training tour at Ft Ord two years earlier. At Ft Leonard Wood, we concentrated on the skills and techniques of infantry combat in Vietnam and the basic survival skills the individual soldier would need there. Rifle marksmanship is a critical skill all recruits have to master. We found that those with some rifle experience often did better initially but never improved. Those with little or no rifle experience but willing to learn improved considerably over their training. We were also teaching a new technique called instinctive firing. It used the technique of skeet shooting, where the shooter used both index fingers to point the weapon at the target instinctively. Every basic training has a recruit that his peers consider slow. In preparation for the instinctive shooting, I would take this recruit out after training and teach him how to shoot. We used air rifles and large aluminum discs that were thrown in the air about ten feet in front of the shooter. After a few days, this recruit could hit a small disc every time. On the first day of training for instinctive shooting, I would call out this particular recruit for a demonstration. When he hit the small disc three times in a row, all the other recruits assumed this was an easy skill. They were right if they followed the instruction and practiced. It was also the shooting more common in combat operations in Vietnam.

One of my more challenging assignments was to receive a full allocation of 200 recruits from "McNamara's 100,000." These were men that had previously been evaluated as unsuitable for the draft. Some were physically unqualified, while others were educationally handicapped. The five platoons of 40 soldiers each were segregated by need: PT, reading and writing, and general.

Some very intelligent young men were in atrocious physical condition. Where we could, we improved their physical conditioning to the point where they could actually pass the Physical Fitness Test (PFT). I was surprised to lead PT as a 25-year-old with 18- and 19-year-olds unable to do push-ups or sit-ups. Those who never could pass the PFT moved on to some other phase or were administratively discharged.

For various reasons, many physically fit young men had never completed the required number of grades in school and were functionally illiterate. Most of these recruits eventually learned enough to pass all the written exams, and many became good soldiers. I can remember holding a reading class on more than one Saturday morning. These were some of my most enjoyable teaching moments, watching young men experience the joy of reading for the first time.

The workdays were long, and weekend duty always seemed to continue. It was a time of turmoil in the Army as the ***Big Green***

*Machine* geared up to send more and more soldiers to Vietnam. It did not take a genius to realize I would soon face a second tour there. The challenge: how best to be a successful infantry officer while caring for my family. We decided that if I was to be more in control of my career, the best decision was to go ahead and volunteer. I soon received orders to Vietnam and the 101st Airborne Division.

The plan was for my wife and one-year-old daughter to rent a small house two blocks over from her parents' house. One of the more touching experiences for her was the second visit to the pediatrician she had been referred to for our daughter's pediatric care. At the end of the visit, she asked when the bill for the first visit would be sent. The doctor's secretary said there would be no bill for as long as her husband was in Vietnam. What a wonderfully patriotic and supportive message that pediatrician sent to a young mother on her own with a small child.

# Chapter 4: Commanding an Airborne Rifle Company

On my return to Vietnam in August 1968 and again landing at Tan Son Nhut Air Base, Saigon, I thought, "Well, this time, I know what I am in for and am prepared." I put on my old jungle fatigues and headed to the Replacement Center. On the way to the center, a young lieutenant, clearly just in from the bush, saluted and asked, "Where are you headed, Captain?" I said to the 101[st.] Airborne. He had the strangest look on his face. I am sure he assumed I was headed back to the States. It was also possible that the LT realized for the first time that many of us were coming in-country for the second and third tours, and he would probably be coming back as well.

My orders had been changed (nothing new), and I was now going to the 3rd Brigade, 82nd Airborne. The 3rd Brigade was deployed from Ft Bragg in 1968 in response to the Tet Offensive and relieved the Marines at Hue/Phu Bai, Northern I Corps. While not entirely unhappy with the change as I boarded a C-130 aircraft to Phu Bai. Shortly after landing, I found myself in the hastily prepared administrative section of the 3rd Brigade alongside Phu Bai airfield. I

reported to the Brigade Commander, COL Alexander R. Bolling, Jr. After welcoming me to the Brigade; COL Bolling asked me what I had done during my first tour and what I wanted to do on this tour. After reviewing my previous assignments in Vietnam, I requested to command a rifle company COL Bolling said, "Get your gear and meet me on the helipad in ten minutes." In this picture, I am ready to leave with COL Bolling. After a short helicopter ride west, COL Bolling's command and control helicopter dropped us into a small clearing overlooking part of the Perfume River and one of the critical bridges. Captain Rodriquez, the current commander of Bravo Company, 2nd Battalion, 505th Parachute Infantry Regiment, was waiting on the ground for the helicopter. COL Bolling told Captain Rodriquez to grab his gear; he was relieved and turned to me and said, "There's your company, Captain. The battalion commander will be out to see you shortly. Good luck." Such was my assumption of command of B/2-505. I found the Bravo Company Command Post (CP) and introduced myself to the two RTOs (radio telephone operators) standing watch. When one of them asked why I was there, I told them I was their new company commander. These two young paratroopers were not fazed and welcomed me to Bravo Company. I don't remember meeting the current battalion commander during that first week. I am sure he came out to the company, but who he was and when he was there escaped me.

Bravo Company's primary mission was securing a key bridge over the Perfume River and the surrounding area. It was on Highway 1 and connected the two provinces south of Hue City. During the fierce fighting in 1968, the Marines had to commit a battalion to secure the bridge from the NVA. Within a week, I had platoons patrolling within two kilometers of the bridge on both sides and at least one platoon on the bridge at all times. Two weeks after my arrival, I was outside my tent shaving when a couple of rifle shots from more than 200 meters came in my direction. I later found out that the local VC tried this occasionally to send the message that they were still around. However, the fact that I didn't duck or scurry for cover told the troops that I was indeed a veteran and knew what I was doing (or at least I hoped that's what they thought).

Within the month of my arrival, Bravo Company was "chopped" (in Army terms, that means you are now working for another unit) from the 2/505 and attached to the 2nd Battalion, 327th Infantry, 101st Airborne Division. While we became the orphan company, the rest of the 2nd of the 505th Battalion and the 3rd Brigade moved south by air to Bien Hoa, just north of Saigon. As part of my introduction to the 101st Airborne Division, I met the 2/327 battalion commander, LTC Charlie Beckwith, at a 101st artillery battery position. After coordinating with the company commander of the 2/327th, whose area of operations we assumed, I asked when the battalion commander would be coming in. The company commander pointed to a helicopter on short final and said, "That looks like him right now." A figure stood on the helicopter's left skid and jumped off just as the chopper landed. He approached me and said, "I'm Charlie Beckwith; where's your Ranger Tab?" Within a few minutes, I learned little about the AO and more about Beckwith, particularly his first tour exploits with Special

Forces and how an NVA .52 caliber machine gun had wounded him in the stomach. The exploits of Charlie Beckwith are many, not the least of which is that he is credited with the formation of Delta, the first Special Operations unit.

As the bastard child of 2/327, Bravo Company, 2/505 drew many of the Battalion's shit details. We spent more time in the bush, fewer days securing artillery at firebases, and fewer opportunities to stand down. Finally, after three months with 2/327 and a few unsatisfactory firefights with local VC and NVA, Bravo Company was released to its parent 2/505th Battalion down south.

The plan was that our rear detachment would precede the bulk of the unit, and once the company was released from the 101st, we would fly to Bien Hoa. In the late afternoon, we were trucked to Phu Bai Airfield for transport to Bien Hoa. One C-130 was provided for the entire company of soldiers just coming in from the field, about 120 fully loaded, dirty, and tired paratroopers. The flight crew packed us in the aircraft like sardines.

Fortunately, we landed about 40 minutes later, just after dark. I looked out of the aircraft and asked the pilot where we were. He said, "Da Nang, we ran out of 'crew time' and had to land here." So, one more day before rejoining the Battalion. Since we had no one to meet us and nowhere to go, we set up our poncho liners in the airfield between runways for the night. No need for security, so everyone got a good night's sleep. It was so different than being in the bush. The night was filled with aircraft landing and taking off, and we were on a nicely mowed grassy infield.

Then at dawn on a bright sunny day, a jeep came screaming across the airfield while I was enjoying my C-ration cup of coffee. An Air Force major jumped out and asked, "Just what in the hell are you doing on my airfield?" I happily explained that the Air Force had dropped us off last night, and we were awaiting transportation to Bien Hoa. Quickly we were hustled aboard the first available C-130 and landed at Bien Hoa midmorning. Had DaNang been hit with a ground attack that evening, I would bet no one knew what a robust, rapid

reaction force was available to them. Although DaNang was considered a "safe area," 120 well-armed paratroopers would have made any enemy effort to penetrate the airfield difficult. This photo is immediately after we landed in Bien Hoa and joined the rest of the 2/505th Parachute Infantry Battalion for a couple of days of stand-down before returning to the bush.

My eight months commanding Bravo, 2/505, were highlighted by intense combat, hilarious non-combat events, and a five-day leave in Hawaii with my bride of five years.

During my last month in command, we were assigned an area of operations almost wholly water. To accomplish our mission, we were provided with several boats, motor boats, airboats, and an LCM (landing craft medium) that served as my company command post. This picture captures what it was like to operate in that environment. Preparing to get wet and then staying wet.

After a formal but bittersweet change of command commemorated by this photo, I reported to Brigade Headquarters. I assumed duties as the S-3 Air Operations Officer for the Brigade. While not nearly as rewarding as commanding a unit, the job was exciting because, at any moment, the Brigade had many air assets (rotary wing and fixed wing) assigned to support the combat units. Lieutenant Colonel (LTC) James Irons was the battalion commander receiving the company guidon signifying the transfer of command from me to my successor commander. The reader will

notice I am wearing a 25th Infantry Division patch on my right shoulder. It signifies that I served in combat with the 25th Infantry

Division. Upon leaving Vietnam, I exchanged it for the 82nd Airborne Division should sleeve insignia.

Fairy tale or war story?

# Chapter 5: Ten Days in Combat

In early 1969, while I was commanding Bravo (B) Company, 2nd Battalion, 505th Parachute Infantry Battalion, 3rd Brigade, 82nd Airborne Division, the battalion was placed under the operational control of the 1st Cavalry Division. 2/505, along with the 1st Cav, was to block NVA (North Vietnamese Army) regiments coming out of Cambodia enroute to Saigon. 2/505 was placed on the division's right flank (east), and Bravo Company had the battalion's right flank. Although this sounds quite clear and uncomplicated, the terrain was

Enroute to the LZ and watching the artillery

such that the only contact between companies was by radio, and movement was coordinated by the battalion commander flying above the companies. On January 11, 1969, Bravo Company made a combat assault into a then-unnamed LZ (landing zone) and immediately made contact with the NVA forces, later identified as the 9th NVA Division.

For the next ten days, we intermittently fought small engagements and much larger firefights with an enemy that was both difficult to pin down and, fortunately for us, poorly coordinated. One morning just after the morning patrols had deployed, 1LT Don Paquin, the FO (artillery forward observer), assigned to B company, and I were sitting on our helmets, having just made our C ration coffee (me) and cocoa (Don) when we heard the distinctive plop, plop, plop of mortar rounds leaving their tubes. We looked at each other and together said, "That ain't ours." Grabbing our steel helmets, we hit the ground, pulled out our compasses, and shot compass azimuths to the sound of the mortars. As mortar rounds began falling on our position, we halved each of our azimuths, and Don called for counter-battery fire from our supporting artillery. Unfortunately, the NVA mortar rounds were on target, and we suffered one killed and four wounded that required medevac.

January 16 and 17 were some of the heaviest engagements. At one point, all four platoons were under heavy fire from fortified NVA positions and were effectively pinned down, unable to maneuver. Attempts by Tiger platoon leader 1LT Greg Ellison and Panther platoon leader, 1LT Rock Rykaczewski, to maneuver against the heavy fire resulted in both being killed within minutes of each other. I was initially shaken because I had never lost a platoon leader, and to lose two within five minutes was a blow. Both were outstanding young officers doing what infantry officers do in combat – leading soldiers.

Over the next two hours, we suffered two more killed and eight more wounded. Recognizing that we had lost leadership in the two platoons, I reorganized the company quickly. I led Tiger and Panther platoons to a rear assembly area and set up 360-degree security. Leopard and Weapons platoons continued to receive intermittent fire, but the NVA did not attempt a full-scale attack. Both platoons kept a steady fire against limited enemy efforts to penetrate our lines. The NVA were either unwilling to fully engage or confused about where and how many US troops they faced, so they did little more than send small attacks against us. We then began systematically applying heavy artillery and air strikes against the known positions while getting out our wounded and dead on the medical evacuation (MEDEVAC) helicopters.

First Lieutenant Bob Haddock was serving as the company executive officer in the rear when he learned both platoon leaders had been killed. He jumped on the first resupply helicopter and joined us in the field. I assigned Bob the responsibility for both Tiger and Panther platoons. He served as their platoon leader until we returned to base camp.

Within a day, we stumbled across a bundle of telephone wires strung along a heavily traveled trail. After tapping into the wire, one of our interpreters learned that our earlier counterbattery fire when we were hit with mortars had been quite successful. It destroyed two of the three 82mm mortars and killed a number of the mortar crews. During these intercepted calls, we also learned that we were in the midst of the 9th NVA division and likely within striking distance of at least two regiments of about 2000 NVA soldiers.

I decided, and the battalion commander agreed, that it was the wrong time to take offensive action and that using artillery and air would be a much better way of taking on the enemy units. For the rest of that day and into the night, we had most of the II Corps available artillery and air assets pounding the jungle in all directions. One indication of the enemy's proximity was the foxhole my interpreter had dug for himself. He seemed to have dug himself up to his eyes within minutes of listening to the NVA telephone conversations.

After a day or so of policing the battlefield and collecting anything that might be of intelligence value, we returned to the Brigade base camp at Bien Hoa. That ended for B Company a ten-day operation that saw us lose 12 killed and 18 wounded. Some of the wounded returned to duty, but the more seriously wounded were sent back to the States and hospitals that could better accommodate their injuries. We had a short memorial service for those killed in action and a prayer service for the wounded and their recovery. These two events are significant for many reasons. First, it recognizes the sacrifice of those we lost and reminds us that we have an obligation to remember them. Second, we want the wounded to know that we care for them and wish them well, particularly those that will not return to the company.

Our after-action report reported over 200 NVA killed, with many

more likely carried from the battlefield. We also captured several individual and crew-served weapons. We learned that B Company and 2/505 had inflicted significant losses on the 9th NVA Division. It was later confirmed from captured NVA documents that the 9th NVA Division was combat ineffective for the next 12 months. We also learned later that B Company had been dropped in the middle of the 9th NVA division, and our constant contact with the NVA units disrupted their move ment and caused them to abandon any further movement south toward Saigon eventually. Four Silver Stars, six Bronze Stars with V device, seven Commendation Medals with V device, and 20 Purple Hearts

were awarded to members of Bravo Company for action during those ten days. During the ten days, I was recognized with a Silver Star and a Bronze Star with a V device for my leadership and actions. This picture was taken just after we headed back to base. I'm the guy with the radio stuck to his ear.

# Chapter 6: Lunch at the Air Force Officers Club

In early 1969, after intense fighting along the Cambodian border Bravo Company, 2nd Battalion, 505th Parachute Infantry Regiment, 82nd Airborne Division was airlifted back to its base at Bien Hoa. Describing our attire wasn't difficult; we were "grungy." How grungy? After two weeks without showers or shaving, pushing through the jungle in 100-degree heat and humidity, we smelled, and our jungle fatigues were even dirtier! To add to the grunge factor, we were still fully locked and loaded with our helmets, rifles, pistols, and hand grenades dangling from our web gear. We had not taken a break for showers, and I thought having lunch at the Officers' Club at Ton Son Nhut Air Force Base would be a morale boost for my officers and me.

Ton Son Nhut Airbase was the headquarters of the US Air Forces in Vietnam and the Headquarters of the US Forces in Vietnam. So, the Officer's Club at Ton Son Nhut was the best in Vietnam. There were linen tablecloths, shiny silverware, crystal water glasses, linen napkins, and tuxedo-wearing Vietnamese waiters. Little did they know the officers they would share lunch with that day.

When the five 82nd Airborne officers arrived at the Club entrance in grungy field gear and weapons, we were greeted by an enlisted man acting as a concierge who asked what we were doing at the club. Since we never wore our rank in the field, he assumed we were all enlisted men. I answered with my captain's rank and said that my lieutenants and I had a reservation, and it was that table in the middle of the room with the "reserved" sign on it. He went as white as a sheet and stammered, "But you can't come in here." I assumed he meant "dressed like that." We ignored him as the five of us turned into the dining room.

The dining room was full of Air Force and Army officers at lunch when we entered. All of them were in freshly laundered uniforms, shined jungle boots, and no weapons. When they saw the five of us enter the room, a hush came over the room, and we could feel the eyes following us to the table in the middle. As we arrived at the table, we stowed our helmets under our chairs and slung our web gear and weapons on the back. We ignored the many eyes watching our every move. Our sudden appearance in "their" club would have been similar to a group of firefighters traveling directly from a large fire to a swanky 5th Avenue restaurant in New York. The surprised diners in the Officer's Club could not have been more astonished than diners at that 5th Avenue restaurant.

A full colonel came in and started for our table shortly after we seated ourselves. I learned later that he was the base commander. Seeing the table occupied, he turned and talked with the enlisted man who had first approached us. After some discussion, they agreed we would keep the commander's table for lunch.

I remember a packed lunch of shrimp cocktails, lobster bisque, hamburgers, French fries, and a couple of beers apiece. We enjoyed the opportunity to experience food not eaten out of a can with a plastic spoon and washed down with tepid water. I remember the Vietnamese waiters enjoyed our generous tips. We always smile when remembering how those rear detachment folks, both Army and Air Force, reacted to the fully locked and loaded officers from the 82d Airborne. Even after fifty-plus years, officers from the 82nd Airborne still talk about that lunch and the "balls" it took to take over the base commander's table in the Ton Son Nhut Officers Club.

In retrospect, this lunch experience illustrated how differently Vietnam veterans served. Some spent their time in the jungles and rice paddies, and others on secure bases in support operations. As with all wars, those who can make the best of their circumstances always do so. Likewise, when another group takes advantage of those circumstances, even briefly, there is shock and awe. For many of those officers, it may have been the first time they saw "grunts," an affectionate name applied to all those dirty, sweaty, smelly infantrymen at the point of the spear.

# Chapter 7: The Legend of the "Duckhunter"

In all branches of the military certain individuals make a name for themselves. Sometimes that name has more to do with something they did than anything else. So, it was with First Lieutenant Donald Paquin. Don was attached to my infantry company in 1969 as the Forward Observer (FO). The role of an FO is to serve as the fire support coordinator for the infantry unit he supports. This meant he could call for artillery support from his own artillery unit and artillery and air support from any and all available units.

Don was a very interesting officer. He joined the Army and became a Special Forces, noncommissioned officer, serving in Vietnam in 1966. In 1967, he applied to Warrant Officer flight training and was sent to Ft Rucker, Alabama, to learn how to fly helicopters. On his first attempt to fly a helicopter, he recounts how the instructor told him he was the worst candidate he had ever had and would never learn how to fly. Don was then given a choice; either go back to being a noncommissioned officer or go to Officer Candidate School (OCS). He opted for OCS and ended up at Ft Sill, Oklahoma, the home of the field artillery. Although disappointed that he could not become an aviator, he soon found that blowing up things and getting paid for it was well worth the effort to get through OCS.

Don had been with my company for a number of months when the company was provided with a ground radar unit. This was to provide early warning of enemy activity beyond our current observation abilities. While these units were in the experimental phase, there was much optimism about their effectiveness. The radars were most active at night, and one particular night was no exception. One of the operators found Don Paquin and excitedly told him they had identified a large unit moving toward our positions. Don woke me, and we both watched the radar returns and realized there was a large concentration on the radar screen, and it was clearly moving in our direction. The radars were supposed to do this, and we began to prepare for the worst.

To Don, this obvious enemy formation was a target to be engaged with all available firepower. Don immediately called supporting artillery fire. After about an hour, the large radar signature was gone. We looked forward to sending up a helicopter at first light to determine the results of our engagement with the enemy formation.

At first light, the helicopter from the Brigade aviation section overflew the area that we had identified on the radar. Upon reaching the area, the pilot radioed back, "They are all dead ducks." Our immediate thoughts of success were dashed when he said, "I meant there are all dead ducks." Once at the location where the radar had identified this large enemy unit, we found a flock of many ducks. They must have been moving overland, sometimes walking and sometimes flying from one area to another. Meanwhile, the question was how to dispose of all the "dead ducks?"

We called on the engineers attached to the Brigade for advice and assistance. Initially, the use of bulldozers to bury the ducks was discarded because the area was all rice paddies, and the dozers would get stuck. Don suggested that the ducks could be burned if they had flame throwers, and nothing would be left. The engineers rounded up a couple of flame throwers and incinerated the duck carcasses. Unfortunately, not all the ducks were dead. In fact, many of them could fly. And fly, they did! Those who could take off with feathers in flames headed for the nearest village. Ducks landing on top of coconut palm houses with burning feathers started some fires that the engineers and the villagers quickly put out.

The story's epitaph is that the United States Army reconsidered using ground radars. And, because Don Paquin was calling for the artillery on the ducks, he became known as "The Duckhunter." That moniker is now part of the folklore of the 82nd Airborne Division, particularly within the division's artillery units. Until Don passed away in 2021, he was remembered by his comrades in arms as the Bravo Duckhunter. While this story recounts the event, no one could tell the story quite like Don Paquin.

# Chapter 8: Back to Fort Benning, Home of the Infantry

Upon my return from Vietnam in 1969 and after a long airplane

ride and three weeks of vacation, the Army sent me to Fort Benning, Georgia, for the Infantry Officers Advanced Course.

Ft Benning, the home of the Infantry. Because I arrived at Benning too late for one class and too early for the next, I spent two months as a "platoon advisor" for the Infantry Office Basic Course. Before joining my Infantry Officer Advanced Course class, the Army called it a "snowbird" assignment. The point of assigning combat veterans to the basic course was to provide the new lieutenants with a better understanding of what they could expect when they reached their units in Vietnam. My most memorable experience one month was appearing before a review board for one of the lieutenants. This lieutenant was a University of Georgia ROTC grad and could not pass a written test to save his life. He played football at Georgia, and according to him, he was there to play football and apparently learned very little while in college. After college, he played nose guard for two years for the Atlanta Falcons when the Falcons first joined the NFL. He said that after two years of playing nose guard and getting beaten up every Sunday, the infantry couldn't be anything but better. He excelled in all the fieldwork and aced the land navigation and leadership courses. But because he couldn't pass the written tests, the board had to decide if he would be retained on active duty. The President of the Board asked me if I would take him as one of my platoon leaders in combat, and I answered, "In a heartbeat, yes, sir." I often wonder how the lieutenant did and where he is now.

Toward the end of the nine-month course, we received our follow-on assignments. I will not forget Jack Todd's face when he returned from his phone call to Infantry Branch assignments. He said, "I'm going back to Nam. They told me I went from being a captain with two tours to a major with none." Jack and I served in the 3rd Brigade, 82nd Airborne Division. He commanded A Company 2-505, and I commanded B Company 2-505. I later learned that he spent his third year in Vietnam as a battalion advisor with the Vietnamese Airborne Division and, although involved in some of the fiercest fighting, came home in one piece.

On the other hand, I could not believe my luck when I received my next assignment. I was going to an ROTC assignment at my alma mater – Eastern Kentucky University, in Richmond! Only two hours from my wife's parents in Sellersburg, Indiana. We

were looking forward to this new assignment and were astonished that the Army had agreed to my request for ROTC duty. More recently, Ft Benning has been renamed Ft Moore.

# Chapter 9: Reserve Officer Training Corps (ROTC) and NOK and SAO Duties

Upon arriving in Richmond and joining the ROTC Detachment at Eastern Kentucky University, I found that my perspective on the university differed significantly from when I was a student. Being a student, one gets the impression of "looking in" on the organization. Once you are a part of it, you spend more time "looking out" at what is happening around the university. ROTC duty at Eastern was the best of both worlds; it was a solid and active detachment of more than 15 officers and enlisted and a supportive academic environment. Classes were challenging for the cadets, and other opportunities for me presented themselves on campus.

Besides teaching courses and two long summer camp sessions, ROTC instructors routinely served as Next of Kin (NOK) notification officers and Survivor Assistance Officers (SAO) in their region of the country. Those detailed as the NOK were never the SAO for that same family because it made the SAO's job easier. The officers in the ROTC detachment were on a duty roster for both NOK and SAO duties. When a NOK assignment was received at the ROTC detachment, the officer and NCO on call would leave immediately. The Department of Defense's goal was to have the notification made within 24 hours of positive fatality identification.

During 1970 and 1971, I had the intimidating task of pulling several NOK and SAO duties. All duties were sobering because the notification and assistance were almost always for soldiers killed in action in Vietnam. Some were incredibly challenging. One NOK detail required the NCO and I to travel to a farmhouse a few miles from Danville, Kentucky. When I approached the front door, I noticed it was open, and the screen door was latched on the inside. When I knocked on the screen door, a male voice from inside said clearly, "Get off my porch." After I said that I was here on official government business and needed to speak to Mrs. So and So, the voice again said, "Get off my porch." This time the demand was punctuated by the twin barrels of a shotgun pressed against the screen. I stepped backward off the porch and went back to the sedan.

We then drove into town, found the local Sheriff, explained why we were there, and were escorted back to the home. It seemed that the spouse of the soldier killed in Vietnam was living with his parents, and the father knew full well why I was there and refused to accept my presence. The wife and the soldier's parents were grief struck when we returned, and the Sheriff didn't even have to come into the house for me to deliver my awful message formally.

On one occasion, while serving as an SAO, I had a funeral detail from Ft Knox that consisted of young men from Minnesota, all tall, blond, and blue-eyed. Their responsibility was to act as pallbearers for the funeral in a small church deep in the mountains of southeastern Kentucky. The church was small, barely wide enough to place the casket in the only aisle and have the pallbearers stand beside it. There were probably 50 people in that little church. Shortly into the service, things got loud, and people started falling on the floor and hollering. Well, that's how "Holy Roller" church folks worship, and those noises and movements were demonstrations of their faith. The six young men standing alongside the casket (probably raised as Lutherans) were unnerved. While their eyes grew, I looked at each of them from the back of the church and mouthed repeatedly, "Stand Fast!" "Stand Fast!"

After the minister said some final words and the congregation gathered itself, we moved outside, almost right around the corner of the church entrance to the gravesite. I choked a little as I presented the flag to the parents. Although many of us have seen this being done, the experience of handing the folded flag to a grief-stricken mother, father, or wife is one of the hardest things I have ever done. It mattered not how many times I did this; each one was as hard as the first.

Although I had briefed the funeral director, the preacher, and the family about the bugler and the 21-gun salute, everyone hit the ground as soon as the first volley went off. I mean everyone, the family, the guests, the preacher, and the funeral director. The guys in uniform were the only ones still standing. As everyone regained their feet and dusted themselves off, little smiles of chagrin were all around. To the soldier's credit, not a one cracked a smile.

On a separate NOK, my NCO and I traveled to a farm deep in southwest Kentucky. A seven-year-old girl was playing in the yard when we arrived at the address. When she saw us, she ran to the car and said, "Do you know my brother? He is in the Army, too?" Of course, that was the soldier killed in Vietnam, and we were there to notify his parents. We asked if her parents were home. She replied. "They are out at the barn." She then jumped into the back seat of the military car and said, "I'll show you how to get there." She directed us to the road that led to a large barn. At the barn were her parents, who looked much older than we expected. As I approached the pair, the mother slumped into a chair, and the father sat down. As soon as I finished my quick delivery of the most awful words a parent could hear, both parents fainted, and the little girl ran off. The NCO and I were left with two barely conscious parents and no idea where the little girl had gone.

The little girl had run to her older brother's farm and told them what she had just heard. Fortunately, the older brother came speedily and helped his parents recover. We explained that a Survivor Assistance Officer (SAO) would be in touch shortly to assist the family.

Although this NOK duty was not our first and would not be our last, the face of that seven-year-old is one you do not forget. I am certain there were other memorable NOK and SAO experiences. These left the greatest marks on my memory.

# Chapter 10: Germany and the Third Infantry Division (3ID)

After so much time away from the Army in the field, I needed to return to an infantry unit. After some badgering of the infantry assignments officer, the assignment soon came through; 3d Infantry Division in Germany.

My arrival in the Division could have been better timed, as the G2 was also the acting Chief of Staff. He had made a deal with the Commanding General to serve as the Chief of Staff if the next combat arms Captain sent to the division would be assigned as his G2 Operations Officer. I was that combat arms Captain and, much to my dismay, got that job instead of an assignment to an infantry battalion. My duties were to ensure that the G2 section was always ready to deploy when ordered, that all anticipated enemy Order of Battle (OB) scenarios were ready and that the section kept the division informed of all necessary intelligence. Since 3ID had the Army's first division-level "all source" intelligence center, we were continuously being watched to see how well we performed in this new concept. One aspect of being an "all source" intelligence center was receiving intelligence previously available only at the theater or national level.

During the 1973 Yom Kippur War in the Middle East, we knew the Soviet Union had alerted its airborne forces and positioned them at airfields. When we received notification that the aircraft had taken off, it triggered a great deal of concern at the headquarters UNTIL one of the junior analysts recognized that the aircraft was not pressurized and that if, in fact, there were paratroopers aboard, they were dead. Tension dropped considerably after that.

Shortly after MG Walker left, MG E.C. "Shy" Meyer assumed command of the 3ID. Interviews were held to select the Commanding General's senior Aide de Camp. I agreed to be nominated, and MG Meyer selected me. The duties of the Aide were quite simple: coordinate everything about the Commanding General's schedule and make sure that he was where he needed to be when he needed to be there. Along the way, ensure that he is provided with everything he needs to do his job and that the right people are there when he needs them. Sounds easy, right? 1LT Jim Godwin was selected as the junior or social aide. He and I got along well and worked that time together as a team. The year spent as the aide was one of my broadest educational opportunities in the first ten years of service. MG Meyer was an incredible leader who spent much of his time visiting units and personally working to improve the Division's capabilities and morale. The peacetime Army circa 1973-1976 was a shell of its former wartime self. The new all-volunteer force was just being implemented. Many Vietnam veterans were still on active duty, with no experience other than Nam. Later, while he was the Army Chief of Staff, GEN Meyer would call it the "Hollow Army."

Some of the more memorable experiences involved MG Meyer's "Soldier of the Day" program. Once a week, each battalion-size unit in the division was required to nominate an E4 or below to spend the day with the CG. The units' Command Sergeant Majors (CSM) selected the soldier and were responsible for getting the soldier to division headquarters before 0600. After a short meeting with CSM Tracey, the Division Command Sergeant Major, the soldier met with the CG and then traveled with the CG the entire day. I often had to ask senior officers to move over to let the soldier of the day sit next to the CG during classified and unclassified briefings. By the end of the day, the soldier would have seen and done almost everything the CG did; then, after a short private session with the CG and a debrief from CSM Tracey, the soldier was driven or flown back to his unit.

The long-term effects of that program are hard to quantify. Still, I know that the short-term benefits were a better understanding by individual soldiers of what the CG spent his time doing and how that information was spread throughout the unit. After forty or so weeks of soldiers participating in the program, the improvement in the morale of the division was almost palpable.

The Aide's job was not without stress and tough times. Shortly before the anniversary of his year in command, MG Meyer received notice from the Chief of Staff of the Army that he would be promoted to Lieutenant General and rotate back to Washington as the Deputy Chief of Staff for Operations (DCSOPS) for the Army.

MG Meyer fully expected to spend two years in command and was unprepared for a quick departure after 13 months. For the next two weeks, I suffered the brunt of his disappointment. Nothing I did was correct; it was my fault if anything went wrong. At the end of the two weeks, he called me into the office and apologized for putting me through what he described as his worst two weeks in command. Shortly after that, I came out on the Major's promotion list and began to consider my next assignment.

Just before MG Meyers departed, I was promoted and reassigned to the Division Support Command (DISCOM) as the S1 or Adjutant. This picture shows COL Galvin and Barbara pinning on the Major's oak leaves.

Working for then Colonel Jack Galvin was one of my more enjoyable assignments. Although an infantry officer, COL Galvin commanded a composite brigade-sized unit that included a division-level transportation, full division maintenance battalion, a supply battalion, a medical battalion, a Military Police Company, a Finance Company, and an Adjutant General Company.

Not long after he took command, the Executive Officer (XO) left, and COL Galvin asked me to be the DISCOM XO, a job I held as a newly promoted Major until we left in June 1976.

At MG Meyer's urging, COL Galvin's 3ID DISCOM tested what would become the Army standard for logistical support for an infantry division. The combat service support battalion was reformed into Forward Support Battalions (FSB), which included supply and maintenance and deployed with each maneuver brigade. A main support battalion (MSB) was formed to provide backup for the three FSBs. The after-action report for REFORGER '75 spoke to the success of this demonstrated concept and was the basis for this configuration becoming Army doctrine.

An enjoyable pastime in Germany was participating in "volksmarches," or people walks. These were sponsored by individual villages, with each route of ten and twenty kilometers intended to show off the best attributes of the locale. The villages also competed with the most intricate and ornate medals awarded.

This picture shows our then three-year-old daughter with me on one of those volksmarches. If we walked ten kilometers, she received a gold medal while I received a silver.

# Chapter 11: Inspector General, Battalion, and Brigade in Four Years at Ft Ord

After eleven years, the return to Ft Ord, California, was an assignment novelty. Instead of a young Lieutenant's first assignment, I was now a field grade officer with only one boss – the one-star Commanding General, CDEC. CDEC, the Army's Combat Development and Experimentation Command, was as unique a unit as you can get in the Army. Its mission was to develop and test new weapons systems, select the best then determine the most expedient deployment process.

The work as the Inspector General (IG) at CDEC (Combat Developments Experimentation Command) was interesting but manageable. I heard complaints, conducted unit inspections, and, when necessary, advised the CG on issues that he may or may not have known about. The command was split between Headquarters at Ord and the operational units at Ft Irwin, about two hours away in the desert.

I traveled to Ft Irwin about once a week unless we were in the midst of longer annual unit inspections. My annual inspection team comprised full-time inspectors from the 7th Infantry Division IG's office, augmented with NCOs from CDEC.

Any soldier or civilian employee had the right to submit a complaint to the IG. If the complaint had merit, the IG was required to investigate. If it involved criminal wrongdoing, I reported it to the local Criminal Investigative Command (CID) office. If the activity involved suspected problems with the chain of command, I reported my findings to the highest level in the chain for resolution. Sometimes that was the CG, but more often, it was either a staff director or unit commander within CDEC.

When soldiers submitted complaints, I required they be in writing before meeting with me. One young sergeant, E5, complained that his chain of command was harassing him and a friend, coincidentally being court-martialed at the courtroom down the street. After reading the complaint and hearing the soldier, I looked at his uniform. I noticed he was wearing a combat patch on his right shoulder and awards and decorations rarely seen on soldiers of his youth and inexperience. It did not take long to determine that the soldier had "spruced up" his uniform in order to impress the jury when he testified as a character witness for his friend. After I had notified the Staff Judge Advocate (SJA) of my findings, he called the soldier to the stand during the ensuing court-martial. He asked a very simple question, "Why are you not wearing the ribbons and shoulder sleeve insignia you were wearing yesterday?" I suspect his testimony as a character witness was considered less than credible. My report to the sergeant's company commander likely produced something more lasting for him.

I also received complaints from those outside CDEC who had problems with something or someone in CDEC. One such complaint was from a retired Sergeant Major living outside Ft Irwin. He complained that during one of our tests involving A-10 aircraft, the aircraft "buzzed" his home. I met with the squadron co mmander, who assured me that although their "loiter" area was near the home, they were not "buzzing" the house. Not long after that, I received another letter from the Sergeant Major, and this time, he included a photograph taken inside his living room looking out the window. The picture window was filled with an A-10 aircraft. I took the photo to the squadron commander and suggested that  his pilots might not tell him the truth. Needless to say, it never happened again.

After I completed the mandatory two-year duty as an IG, I looked for an infantry assignment in the 7ID there at Ord. The infantry branch supported this move, and I reported to the 3$^{rd}$ Battalion, 32$^{nd}$ Infantry, 3$^{rd}$ Brigade, 7ID as the Executive Officer. The battalion commander, Clancy Matsuda, and I hit it off from the beginning. I was getting my feet wet with all the responsibilities of a battalion executive officer when Clancy went to DC for over three months on a promotion board. For almost the next four months, I served as the acting battalion commander of 3-32. While the 7ID was classified as a "light infantry" division, each maneuver battalion had 256 vehicles. This required a considerable maintenance effort, and much of my time was spent ensuring that the line companies conducted the required maintenance.

Shortly after Clancy's return from DC, I was selected for promotion to Lieutenant Colonel. Almost immediately, Division Headquarters reassigned me to Headquarters, 1st Brigade, 7th Infantry Division (7ID) as the Executive Officer. My assumptions about why I might have been selected were supported by the fact that the 7th ID Commander was MG Phillip R. Feir, my former battalion commander in my first Vietnam tour. He had pulled me from a rifle company in Vietnam to be his battalion logistics staff officer, S-4.

COL Carly Alton, the 1st Brigade commander, was an interesting individual. When I took over as his Executive Officer, his wife was diagnosed with breast cancer. COL Alton spent much time with his wife at home or at the cancer centers for treatment. As a result, many of the brigade command responsibilities fell to me – the new executive officer and still a major. My challenges were initially with the three battalion commanders. All of them were Lieutenant Colonels, and I was not yet promoted to Lieutenant Colonel. Because battalion command is a centrally selected process, it was not surprising that some had large egos. After all, they had been through Staff College, probably commanded in Nam, had great files, and were selected by a panel in DC! Much of my time was spent managing the brigade staff, a mix of inexperienced younger officers and "old guard" guys biding their time to retirement. I hope I handled most decisions correctly. One in particular stays with me:

I received a call late one night from the S2, a senior major, obviously drunk and almost incoherent. It soon became clear that he was distraught about his family situation and seriously considering suicide. I went to his quarters and talked with him, but I don't really remember what I said. I probably just let him talk his way thru it. He did refer himself to the hospital for treatment.

The 1st Brigade, 7ID, deployed to Alaska for a "Brimfrost" exercise in January 1979. As Exec, I led the advance party to Ft Wainwright. Two 1st Brigade battalions, one infantry battalion from the 101st Airborne, and an aviation battalion rounded out the brigade for this exercise. Supervising the soldiers' and unit preparations for cold weather operations and refreshing the brigade's prepositioned  equipment at Wainwright was an 18-hour-a-day job for the better part of a month.

This picture typifies my tour as Brigade XO smiles all around! This was one of the warmer winters in that part of Alaska. It never got colder than 35 degrees below zero. The next winter was one of the coldest. It never got above 35 degrees below zero. One of the dumber things I did while on this exercise was to get lost in the Arctic training area. Environmental concerns required that all Army units completely clean their areas before departing. That meant filling in all holes, removing construction materials, and pulling up all communications wires. Going through one of the battalion areas, I noticed communications wire protruding from a pile of brush. I pulled, tugged, and followed it a long way into the woods, becoming madder and madder at the unit that had failed to comply with the clean-up requirements. Dealing with more and more communications wire, I soon found myself alone in some very deep woods. My jeep and driver were behind me, but I was lost because I had been following the wire and needed clarification on my location. I guess it's true that the good Lord looks after children and fools because I somehow followed the pulled wire and found the way back to my jeep and the driver just before dark. It was a miracle that I made it. The average temperatures at night that winter were 30 below.

Within the next six months, I deployed the brigade to Australia for a joint exercise with the Australian and New Zealand Armies. Those were interesting exercises in the desert "outback," but I remember best the lesson that one should never get into a beer-drinking contest between Aussies and Kiwis.

In late 1980, I realized that if I didn't get selected for battalion command, I would not spend any more time with infantry units. I was on the alternate list when the Battalion command selection list came out. I was disappointed because getting a battalion off the alternate list was rare. With that fact in mind, I planned to continue in intelligence, my alternate specialty, and go on from there.

Discussions with branch assignments were always challenging since, regardless of your request and its logic, the officer making your next assignment primarily tried to fill billets (a big factor in their evaluations). If the two match, you were extraordinarily lucky. I requested an intelligence officer assignment to the Pentagon and the Joint Staff. The assignment officer didn't outright laugh at my request, but his response and tone of voice told me it would be a cold day in hell before that happened. So, it was much to my surprise and good luck when I received orders to the Defense Intelligence Agency (DIA) with duty on the Joint Staff in the intelligence support office for the Chairman of the Joints Chiefs of Staff, JCS. The office abbreviation was DIA-JSJ.

# Chapter 12: SOCCENT and CENTCOM

While serving in the Intelligence Support Office, Chairman of the Joint Chiefs of Staff, JCS, I met Colonel Jerry King, a long-time Special Forces officer. During one of our meetings, he mentioned that he would soon be assigned to US Central Command (CENTCOM) to establish a special operations component. That component would be titled Special Operations Command Central, or SOCCENT. Shortly afterward, he asked if I would move to McDill Air Force Base and become the component intelligence chief, or J2, SOCCENT. I jumped at the opportunity to work for Jerry King and to move to CENTCOM.

SOCCENT was initially very small, with fewer than a dozen officers from all service branches. Our operational units came from Army Special Operations Command at Ft Bragg, including the 3$^{rd}$ and 5$^{th}$ Special Forces Groups. From US Navy Special Warfare Command, including SEAL teams 6 and 8, and from US Air Force Special Operations Wing at Hurlburt Field, Florida. The operational tempo was heavy as the Commander in Chief, US Central Command (CINCENT), pushed hard to establish the command's presence in its Area of Operations (AOR). The AOR included all of North Africa and the Middle East.

Although my assignment to SOCCENT and CENTCOM was supposed to be three years, I spent less than 18 months in Brandon. One example early on was when our oldest daughter graduated from high school in Northern Virginia. Because the family initially stayed in Virginia so she could finish high school, I was already committed to deploying to Kenya. I traveled to Virginia, watched her cross the stage and receive her diploma, and immediately went to Andrews Air Force Base to catch a diplomatic flight to Kenya.

We deployed as a unit to multiple countries in North Africa and the Middle East during my first year at SOCCENT. About halfway through my second year at SOCCENT, I was approached by the Executive Officer to the Commander in Chief if I would consider taking the job of Deputy Executive Officer. After discussing the possibility with Jerry King and getting his approval, I was reassigned to Headquarters, US Central Command, as the Deputy Executive Officer, Office of the Commander in Chief, US Central Command.

My only stipulation for taking the job was that I would remain on jump status for the remainder of the year. I enjoyed the parachute exercises with SOCCENT and maintained my jump proficiency, even though my four-star boss was not enthusiastic about my jump status. General Crist was the first four-star Marine officer named a regional Commander in Chief, or CINC and took that responsibility very seriously.

On December 24, I needed to make a final jump to maintain proficiency and was scheduled late that afternoon with SOCCENT. I checked with the General to ensure he was up to speed on his commitments for Christmas Day and the day after. I made the jump and, just before dark, was headed home. Since this was before cell phones were ubiquitous, I learned he had called my home when I saw

Barbara waiting for me on the front porch. She said, "The general called and needs you back in the office." I turned the car around and went back into the office to find that he had some inconsequential things for me to do. The point was that he gave me one last jab about my jump status and that he did not like our agreement.

Army, Air Force, and Navy promotion lists are always shared with the Commanders-in-Chief before being made public. General Crist called me into his office in early January 1986 and announced, "The Army has screwed up again." I had no clue what he was talking about until he handed me the promotion list for full Colonel and said, "Congratulations." That is how I learned that I would be promoted.

# Chapter 13: Jumping with the Egyptians

During Bright Star '81, I was J2 for Special Operations Command Central (SOCCENT) and deployed with the unit to Egypt as one of the US participant organizations. We joined the 82nd Airborne units that rounded out the US contingent. As part of the exercises, we conducted a number of airborne operations with our counterpart Egyptian paratroopers.

Early one morning, we assembled for the first jump at an airfield outside Cairo, drew our parachutes, and assisted each other in strapping them on. Afterward, each unit was divided equally between US and Egyptian C-130 aircraft. While we sat on the tarmac and waited for the aircraft crew to finish their preflight checks, we noticed that many Egyptian paratroopers were quite excited about the upcoming jump and talked excitedly to each other. "Allah Akbar" was heard many times during those conversations. Typically, the American paratroopers leaned back on their parachutes and took a little nap. In our minds, this was the typical "hurry up and wait" period before anything happened.

Once boarded the aircraft, each group was divided equally into "sticks" between American and Egyptian jumpers. A "stick" is the line of paratroopers to exit the aircraft. On the aircraft's port side, the first fifteen jumpers in the "stick" were Egyptians, and the last fifteen in the "stick" were Americans. On the starboard side, my side, the first fifteen were Americans and the last fifteen Egyptians. As the senior member of the American contingent, I was first in line, or in Airborne terminology, I was "in the door" and the first one to jump on the aircraft's starboard side.

US airborne operations have two key team members: the jumpmaster and the safety. The jumpmaster is responsible for the safe execution of the jump, and the safety assists the jumpmaster primarily by securing the static lines of each jumper as they approach the door. As I stood in the door waiting for the signal to jump, or the green light, I glanced over to the aircraft's port side and noticed that there were four Egyptians in the positions held by the jumpmaster and the safety. I thought nothing of it until after I was on the ground.

The aircraft I jumped from was the last in the line of a flight of four C-130s. As I drifted to the desert floor, I looked for the parachutes of those that had jumped before me. That check aimed to see which way the wind was blowing and make my adjustments to land. The parachutes normally point away from the wind once the jumper has landed. I didn't see many flattened parachutes as I looked down on the desert floor. In fact, I saw many still inflated and pulling their jumper across the desert floor. Fortunately, I landed and quickly hit my quick release which allowed my chute to deflate.

Once the Americans had landed and grouped together for the follow-on activities, many of the group in the aircraft with me were laughing about the antics aboard the aircraft. The Egyptians became quiet as we approached the drop zone and the jumpmaster gave us the five-minute signal. This was quite a contrast from their earlier animated conversations. I also learned the reason for the four Egyptian jumpmasters/safety personnel. Apparently, not all the Egyptian paratroopers were eager to exit the aircraft. According to the Americans in the "stick" behind them, the Egyptian jumpmasters forcefully helped them out the door by grabbing anyone who hesitated and throwing them bodily out of the aircraft. Often this was accompanied by a swift kick in the buttocks.

It was also apparent that few, if any, of the Egyptian paratroopers had been trained to use the parachute quick-release levers. More than a few were dragged across the desert before they could collapse their parachute. One Egyptian was stunned when he hit the ground and was dragged across the desert for a hundred yards. His steel helmet with a cloth camouflage cover was scoured so that a large spot on the back of the helmet was polished to a high shine.

We jumped with the Egyptians a couple more times and found their method for encouraging jumpers remained effective. We also put a drop zone safety officer with the Egyptian on the ground to verify the suitable wind conditions. It seemed that the Egyptian officer on the drop zone needed to learn how to correctly measure the winds on the ground for the first drop. The differences between American and Egyptian training and professionalism were very apparent.

Fairy tale or war story?

# Chapter 14: How I Saw the Challenger Tragedy

In 1986 I was with Special Operations Command, Central (SOCCENT) based at MacDill Air Force Base outside Tampa, Florida. As the Special Operations component of the US Central Command, we were an airborne unit with the mission of conducting special operations within the geographic area of responsibility of the US CENTRAL Command. As an airborne unit, we conducted numerous airborne operations in the US and in our assigned countries. We also worked closely with other US Army, Air Force, and Navy Special Operations units.

In January 1986, SOCCENT was scheduled to participate in a joint special operations exercise with the 3rd and 5th Special Forces Groups stationed at Ft Bragg, North Caroline. To initiate the exercise, SOCCENT members would fly from MacDill Air Force Base and conduct an airborne operation into Ft Bragg. Early on January 26, 1986, I boarded a C-130 aircraft with other unit members and headed northeast toward Ft Bragg.

Not long after takeoff, the pilot came to the aircraft's rear and told us that the Challenger space shuttle was in the final countdown for liftoff at Cape Canaveral. He told us to look out the aircraft's starboard (right) side, and we could see the shuttle take off.

As many of us as we could crowded around the aircraft's windows and watched as the Challenger lifted off from Cape

Canaveral. Our aircraft cruised at about 35,000 feet, and we could see the Challenger liftoff. Just about the time it reached an altitude 10,000 feet above us, it exploded. We watched as pieces of the shuttle fell and the booster rockets went off in different directions.

There was absolute silence on the aircraft as we tried to process what we had just witnessed. We asked the pilot if he had learned anything about the shuttle, and he told us that no information was available.

By this time, we were within twenty minutes of our scheduled drop time at Ft Bragg, and we began our inflight parachute rigging and preparation for the parachute jump. We all made the jump and landed without any issues. Once we could, we asked personnel on the ground if they knew what had happened to the Challenger. Unfortunately, they had no more information than we did and were surprised that we had witnessed the Challenger's fate.

Much later in the exercise, we learned that the Challenger had failed due to a faulty seal. We also learned that we were one of the very few who had been within ten thousand feet and ten miles at the exact moment of the explosion. As with other memorable events, one seldom forgets that bright, chilly day in Florida when the Challenger space shuttle and its crew were lost.

# Chapter 15: The United States Army Attaché in London

Within a week after I learned I would be promoted to full Colonel, I received a call from Colonels Branch in the Army Personnel Office. In a hushed tone, the assignments officer told me I was being nominated for a "Black Book" assignment. I had to ask what that meant and learned that it was an assignment that the US Army Chief of Staff had to approve personally. The assignment was approved, and I learned I would be assigned as the US Army Attaché to the Court of St James, United Kingdom, with duty at the American Embassy in London, UK.

Because my assignment called for a full Colonel and I would not be promoted before I reported to the Embassy, the Army authorized that I was "frocked" to my new rank. "Frocking" was being pinned with the new rank but not being paid at that rank until the actual promotion date. In my case, I was a Colonel but was paid as a Lieutenant Colonel.

After a six-week "charm school" in Washington, we left for London and an amazing three-year assignment. The assignment as an Army Attaché was different from any other Army assignment! First, all military assigned to the embassy are diplomatic personnel with the same rights and responsibilities as any Foreign Service officers. The short "charm school" course I attended in DC did little to prepare us for the large diplomatic community we met in London. Second, all the support systems are now embassy centric. The support system a military officer is familiar with, like post housing, the commissary and PX, and a personnel support center, does not exist. Finally, we learned that understanding the scope of "representational" duties and doing them are two different things.

My "duty uniform" was a suit. In contrast, most military functions would be formal affairs requiring dress uniforms, either mess dress or mess whites. As such, I arrived in London with eight three-piece suits, a tuxedo, and both mess dress and mess white in addition to the standard blue and service A uniforms. None of them are in any uniform allowance.

When I arrived, the Assistant Army Attaché, LTC Tom Sanders, had been on station for two years and was a tremendous help during that first year. Tom's advice and counsel were always outstanding, but sometimes I didn't get it right.

We were invited to the Chinese Attaché's home for dinner shortly after our arrival. Tom cautioned me that there would be many courses, so I had better pace myself. Dinner that night was at a large round table with the male guests to the left and right of the host and the female guests to the left and right of his wife. In the center of the table was a large lazy susan filled with many dishes. After the host and hostess served our plates with the selections, I was asked if I would like another serving. Assuming that this was what Tom meant by many courses, I said I would. Surprisingly, this was the first of seven courses, and I was hard-pressed to finish the sixth and seventh. I learned from that experience to always proceed with caution during dinner!

Not long after our daughters joined us, the family was invited and traveled via attaché car to the Edinburgh Tattoo, an annual weeklong festival of music and marching band performances in Edinburgh, Scotland. The highlight of the visit was the final performance of all the bands. Barbara and I sat in the "Royal Box" with the King and Queen of Norway while the daughters sat in the control room for the lights. The final "tattoo" is held in the courtyard of Edinburgh Castle, followed by an invitation-only reception in the castle. Because the tattoo lasted until about 10:00 pm, the reception didn't begin until close to 10:30. Around 11:30, we started planning to leave and couldn't find our youngest daughter. A quick search of the reception room's nearest locations found her curled up on a pillow seat in a battlement window overlooking the courtyard. This incident remains a family story: losing a daughter in Edinburgh Castle.

A less amusing incident during the tattoo was the UCLA marching band playing "Don't Cry for Me Argentina." How quickly we Americans had forgotten that the British and the Argentinians were at war in the Falklands less than a year before. Some not-so-sensitive Brits booed the UCLA band. I could imagine those college kids trying to understand why their music was not appreciated. This incident exemplifies how relationships can become toxic if not properly coordinated. No one from UCLA had bothered to check with the embassy, and no one at the embassy had reviewed UCLA's playlist.

# Fairy Tales and War Stories

One of the highlights of our tour was visiting the many exchange officers. The exchange officer program was decades old and gave American and British officers unique experiences in their allies' armies. Half of my visits were alone while Barbara accompanied me on the others. Our officers played essential roles during their tours with the British Army, and many contributed significantly to the effectiveness and efficiency of their counterpart units. In one instance, a Quartermaster officer successfully revamped the entire supply system for the BAOR (British Army on the Rhine). The supply system had been notorious for its horrendous inventory accountability and lack of spare parts. Nevertheless, his modernization effort received accolades from the highest levels of the British Army. Moreover, it firmly cemented a relationship that I am certain remains today.

While the US Army does not allow foreign officers to command US soldiers, the British have no such restriction. As a consequence, US Army officers commanded helicopter squadrons, tank squadrons, and even medical units.

After a dining out (dinner with spouses) with another regiment, Barbara and I were driven back to our quarters by the regimental commander's driver. Suddenly, before leaving the Army garrison, we were hit by another car. Fortunately, neither vehicle was going very fast, so the damage was minimal, and no one was hurt. However, the Regimental Commander's driver was inconsolable and repeatedly said, "He is going to can me, he is going to can me."

To make matters worse, the driver of the car that hit us was another regiment member who was intoxicated and almost unable to stand. When he realized whose car he had hit, he almost passed out on the spot and was sitting by the side of the road when the military police arrived. I assured the CO that his driver was not at fault and that he did all he could to avoid the collision. I later learned that the NCO at fault soon became a private.

The Tower of London is the traditional regimental home of the Royal Fusiliers, better known as the "Beef Eaters." Early in the tour, I learned that the Continental Army had captured the regimental colors at the battle of Camden during our Revolutionary War. The regimental secretary was eager to make my acquaintance and always asked if there was a way to have the colors returned to the regiment.

Unfortunately, I found that the colors were hanging in the chapel at West Point, and the chances of them being returned were slim and none. However, that did not deter the regimental secretary, and he consistently honored my requests for special tours of the Tower whenever we had family or friends visit us.

Representational duties of an Army Attaché required attendance and hosting many social events. This picture was taken just before we left for "another Christmas party" in 1988. During our final year in London, Barbara and I attended over

250 receptions individually or together. We hosted 30 dinners in our home and 24 receptions. Our representational budget that year was maxed out. We even used some of the Air Force, and Navy attaches budgets. The purpose of these events is to get to know the host country's leadership and to be able to tell the US Army and US defense stories.

Many social events over the three years stood out. We had the occasion to visit Buckingham Palace on three separate occasions, one garden party and two diplomatic receptions. At the first reception, we went through the receiving line that included the Queen, Prince Phillip, Prince Charles, and Princess Diana. As Barbara and I danced with the Queen's orchestra playing on a balcony above us, we looked at each other and said almost simultaneously, "What are two kids from Kentucky doing here?"

On another occasion, the Duke of Cambridge gave us a tour of his estate at a garden party he hosted. During the tour, he mentioned a particular mulberry bush that was often climbed by Queen Elizabeth when she visited as a child. I asked how often she returned to the house, and he quietly informed me that he meant "The first Queen Elizabeth."

We were fortunate to have a close relationship with the vicar of St. Johns Hyde Park, the nearest Anglican Church to our residence. The vicar, Thaddeus Birchard, was an ex-pat American from Louisiana who told us his bishop thought he could do better in the UK and suggested serving the church there. Our youngest daughter started her confirmation classes at St John's and was scheduled to be confirmed on Thanksgiving weekend, 1988. We had already planned a trip to Cairo, Egypt, to visit friends, so we asked Thaddeus if she could be delayed a week or two. He agreed and arranged to have our daughter confirmed with another class. Unbeknownst to us, that class was going to be confirmed at Westminster Abbey by the Bishop of London.

There were more celebrants and choir members than confirmands and family members. Our daughter was quite unruffled by the pomp and circumstance and likely assumed this was how it was always done in London. It was a big deal for the only two American parents in attendance.

# Chapter 16: The Kermit Roosevelt Lectures

One of the annual events enjoyed by both the US Army and British Army military leadership is the Kermit Roosevelt Lectures. President Teddy Roosevelt had four sons, all of whom fought in World War I and two in World War II. The youngest, Quentin, was killed in aerial combat in France in 1918. Kermit, the second son, fought in both WWI and WWII. He joined the British Army in 1914 and then joined the US Army when the US entered the war. He eventually died during WWII in Alaska while deployed with the US 7th Division to repel the Japanese invasion of the Aleutians. The oldest, Theodore Junior, and Archie, the third son, were seriously wounded in WWI. Theodore Junior was also the only general officer on Omaha Beach on D-Day and was awarded the Medal of Honor for his bravery. He died of a heart attack two weeks later. Archie served in the infantry if both WWI and WWII. He received many awards for valor and seven Purple Hearts for his wounds. He is the only serviceman considered totally disabled from both WWI and WWII.

The Kermit Roosevelt Exchange Lecture Series began in 1947. The idea for an annual exchange of American Army and British Army military lecturers came from Mrs. Kermit Roosevelt to memorialize her late husband. The US Army Attaché in London was to both manage the administrative details and escort the British lecturer on his tour in the US. Likewise, the British Army Attaché in Washington escorted the senior Army officer lecturer on his tour in the United Kingdom.

# Fairy Tales and War Stories

I was fortunate to accompany three extraordinary British officers, General Sir John Chapple, General Sir Charles Huxtable, and Field Marshall Sir Richard Vincent. Traveling with them across the country from West Point, Leavenworth, and Washington was a great way to get to know them and their wives personally. As a result, the access I was provided in the Ministry of Defence made my job much easier every year.

When escorting General Chapple, we stopped at US Forces Command Headquarters in Atlanta, Georgia, to visit then-commander General Colin Powell. General Powell's staff organized a dinner party in downtown Atlanta at the Sun Dial restaurant. There were about twelve in the party, in addition to General and Lady. Chapple. When it came time to order the wine, General Powell deferred to General Chapple. General Chapple always had a wry sense of humor and told General Powell that I was a wine aficionado and should select the wine. He knew full well that I was not, and he was having a little fun with me. Fortunately, among the many wines available in the fifty-page listing, I found one I knew from the Cavalry and Guards Club in London, where General Chapple and I were members. When the sommelier brought the wine for me to taste, I found that the taste was off. As only a Frenchman can do, the sommelier said it was impossible. He called the manager, and we opened another bottle of the same wine. When they both agreed that the initial bottle was "bad," everyone at the table had to try a sip to distinguish a good from a "bad" bottle. It made for a story General Chapple later told everyone who would listen.

General Chapple again demonstrated his wry sense of humor during our tour of Arlington National Cemetery. While there, we visited President Kennedy's and his brother Robert's graves. Lady Chapple then asked the guide where the younger brother Ted would be buried. General Chapple quickly quipped, "He has already been buried at Chappaquiddick, my dear." Upon retirement, General Chapple was promoted to Field Marshall and appointed the Director General of Gibraltar. He invited us to visit, and we regret that we never accepted his invitation.

On a later Kermit Roosevelt tour, Field Marshall Vincent, British Chief of Defence Staff, was scheduled for a private meeting with now Chairman of the Joint Chiefs Colin Powell. While waiting in the anteroom, he broke off a button from his service uniform. I quickly grabbed a paper clip and provided a quick repair. This was a technique I learned as a young lieutenant when the laundry would routinely break a button on my field uniform. I don't think the Field Marshall had ever had to replace a button on a uniform in his more than thirty years of service. He was amazed that there was such a simple, temporary solution.

Those fifteen-day tours with senior British Officers were a highlight of the tour. The US Army Chief of Staff provided an aircraft for each tour. I became quite comfortable with the pilot and I planning our trips and deciding when to leave. That must be like having your own plane and going when and where you want without considering the cost.

# Chapter 17: Lockerbie and the PANAM 103 Bombing

On December 21, 1988, I served as the US Army Attaché at the US Embassy in London. On that date, I was the "on call" officer for the Defense Attaché Office, a duty that rotated between the three principal Attaches Army, Navy, and Air Force. I was watching the news at 6:15 that evening when the broadcast of the crash of PANAM 103 was announced. I knew at that moment that I was going to be busy for the next few days.

A quick phone call to the Air Force Attaché confirmed that we had a C-130 aircraft on alert at the closest military airfield, and a car would pick me up shortly. I packed a small bag with civilian clothes and left for the Embassy. I secured a satellite phone, spare batteries, and some miscellaneous office supplies that might be needed and left for the Ambassador's residence in Regents Park. I met with Ambassador Price and briefed him on our travel to Carlisle by air and then car to Lockerbie.

Meanwhile, the Deputy Chief of Mission had rounded up the Consular section and had a representative group on the way to the airfield. When a US citizen dies abroad, the consul general takes responsibility for the remains until the next of kin can accept them. Ambassador Price, his wife Carol, and I then proceeded to the airfield and boarded the C-130. Mrs. Price was an experienced public relations professional and made certain that the Ambassador's many on-air TV and radio interviews went well. While Ambassador Price was a very articulate man, there is no doubt in my mind that she coached him quite well.

Once seated on the jump seats in the aircraft, Ambassador Price asked me about the large plastic container in the center of the aircraft. I told him the only aircraft immediately available was a tanker, and the container was aircraft fuel. He looked at me incredulously and asked what would happen if we had a problem with the aircraft. I tried to make a joke and told him that if anything happened, we probably wouldn't know, and it would be over quickly. Our Legal Attaché (FBI) and the local PANAM representative joined us on the flight. As I recall, there were about 15 in total. More members of the consular section would arrive the next day.

The short flight to Carlisle and less than a thirty-minute fast car to Lockerbie had us on-site at 8:45 pm. We initially went to the crater in the town center where the major part of the aircraft impacted. The scene I experienced is one I shall never forget. You could see the jet fuel still burning at the bottom from the crater's edge. I suddenly realized I was standing in the remains of a home that was about waist high. In the next home, the walls were about chest high; on the other side, that home was missing its roof. As I looked across the crater, the same damage was repeated down the block of homes. It was then that I realized that there had been two homes where there was now a crater. It was in these two homes that eight residents of Lockerbie died.

From the crater, we traveled to the site of the scattered portions of the aircraft wreckage. This was also where most of the passengers had fallen when the aircraft broke apart at 35,000 feet. The area was a natural bowl almost a mile and a half in diameter. By the morning of December 22, the Ministry of Defence had mobilized cadets at a British Army and a Royal Airforce training center to assist in the recovery effort. By mid-afternoon, I looked around the landscape, and for 360 degrees, a young soldier or airman was standing alongside a yellow plastic sheet and a small red plastic flag. These cadets were given four-hour shifts throughout the next two days while forensic teams examined and removed the remains of the passengers and crew of PANAM 103. For more than forty-eight hours, the cadets had secured the remains and prevented any predators from disturbing them.

I also went with one of the forensic teams to the forward part of the aircraft that had landed some distance from the rest. This is also the aircraft part most often seen in television broadcasts. An extended version of the taped version will show me in a tan raincoat looking at the inside of the aircraft. That picture was visually disturbing because I was looking at a passenger in the first-class section. He was still in his seat, leaning forward into the seat in front of him and appearing to be just asleep. I later learned that the usual consciousness (PUC) period for explosive decompression at 35000 feet is about thirty seconds—unfortunately, just enough time to realize what had happened.

The three days in Lockerbie were spent coordinating the efforts of the Embassy to recover remains, allow a forensic analysis of the wreckage, and respond to multiple inquiries from intelligence agencies. We also had many visits from key members of the UK government. Prime Minister Thatcher was scheduled to arrive on one such occasion in the morning. Ambassador Price asked me if the Washington intelligence agencies had anything to share with the Prime Minister. The primary reason for asking was that I was now the only one with a working satellite phone.

The helicopter landing pad was up a small hill from where we stayed. I was on the phone with my contact from the Defense Intelligence Agency, who had collated all additional information from the CIA and NSA. Shortly thereafter, we were told Prime Minister Thatcher's helicopter was inbound. As Ambassador Price and I walked up the hill toward the helipad, I repeated each piece of information I was receiving on the phone. The Ambassador greeted the Prime Minister, and while walking down the hill with her, he repeated almost verbatim everything I had just told him on our walk up the hill. I immediately thought, "Wow, what a great memory!" While his conversation with the Prime Minister probably lasted no more than five minutes, it was a highlight for me to be able to contribute in a small way to the ongoing effort.

Upon returning to the Embassy the day before Christmas, I spent a good deal of time writing classified and unclassified reports on what had happened since the night of December 21st. A footnote to the event was that so many Americans had traveled to Lockerbie to pay their respects to those lost that the UK government severely restricted access at the request of the residents of Lockerbie. Only those with Ambassadorial approval were permitted to visit Lockerbie.

Ambassador Price delegated to me that authority to approve military visits. Within a few weeks, a staff member for a senior officer in the US Army called my office to arrange the general's travel to Lockerbie. I told the staff officer I could not approve the trip because the UK government restricted access. The general then came on the phone and told me in no uncertain terms that he didn't care who I was and that he was going to Lockerbie. I responded that he could travel to Lockerbie but that when he arrived, he would be arrested, declared "persona non grata," and put on the next plane back to the States. After a few choice expletives, the general hung up the phone. He never did travel to Lockerbie.

My Army counterparts have gently kidded me that my tour as the Army Attaché in London must have been one long cocktail party. While the representational part of the job was a lot of social interactions, when there is an emergency that requires the movement of people, equipment, and coordination of multiple efforts, the Defense Attaché office is the one the Embassy relies on to get it done. This was never truer than on that fateful day in December 1988.

# Chapter 18: British Army Dining-Ins and More

For those unfamiliar with military terminology, a "dining in" is a dinner attended only by unit officers. A "dining out" includes the spouses and is usually a less rowdy affair.

As the US Army Attaché in London in the late 1980s, I was invited to many British Army unit dining ins. The reason was that during my tenure, more than 75 US Army officers served in British Army units as two-year exchange officers. Many exchange officers served in operational British Army regiments with long and distinguished histories. My experiences in some of these dining-ins were among the highlights of my assignment in England.

### *Pay the Piper*

The regiment's Colonel asked me if I would participate in the morning as the dinner drew to a close at this regimental dining in. Unsure about what he was referring to, I asked what would happen in the morning. He explained that the regiment was encamped in France during the latter period of the Hundred Years' War. One night, the watch officer was negligent in his duties, and the French army was close at hand. The regimental piper happened to see the French advancing and began to play his bagpipes to alert the regiment of the danger. Fortunately for the regiment, it was able to rally and repulse the French advance. Since the regiment's honorary colonel also happened to be the monarch at the time, he decreed that from that day forward, the regiment's officers would stand to without the benefit of a cloak or cap and listen to the piper play. The next day happened to be the anniversary of that event. I watched from a window while the regimental officers stood in formation at dawn without coats or caps while the piper played for an hour. An unusual event I shall not forget.

### *Loyalty to the Crown*

Having attended more than a few dining-ins at British Army units, I knew that a few things happened at each. One of the activities I saw in all the previous dining-ins was at the conclusion of the dinner; the regimental band would play God Save the Queen. Upon the song's first note, all the officers would rise, and the most junior officer would propose a toast to the Queen. While attending a dining-in at one very senior regiment, I was surprised to see none of the regiment's officers rise when the band played God Save the Queen. The officers continued their conversations and their after-dinner drinks. When the opportunity presented itself, I asked the regiment's Colonel why all the other regiments stood while the band played God Save the Queen but not his. As only a senior British officer can, he raised his chin. He stiffly replied, "This regiment has demonstrated its fealty to the crown on so many occasions that the monarch does not require additional tokens."

## *In My Regiment?*

While the US Army is not permitted to have foreign exchange officers in command positions, the British Army has no such restriction. As a result, at least a third of the US Army exchange officers had the opportunity to serve as commanders in British Army units. One US Army armor officer was assigned to the First Royal Tank Regiment of the British Army and commanded one of their squadrons.

I was invited to attend one of their regimental parades and share the reviewing stand with the Honorary Colonel of the Regiment, then Prince, now King Charles III. As the tank units passed by, it was obvious from his uniform that the American officer was the commanding officer of that squadron.

As the tanks continued past the reviewing stand, Prince Charles turned to the regiment's commanding officer and asked, "Who was that chap in the different uniform?" The colonel proudly replied, "That is Major Smith, our American exchange officer." Prince Charles replied, "In my regiment?" He then turned to me and said, "Good chap," smiling.

Later that day, during lunch, Prince Charles invited Major Smith to join him. He spent thirty minutes learning about the differences between the US Army armor units and British Army armor units. There is no doubt that Major Smith gave Prince Charles a thorough tutorial on the capabilities of the US Army's Abrams tank. At the time, the Abrams were far superior to the outdated Challenger tanks of the British Army.

### *We Must Make Our Own*

During my tenure as the Army Attaché in London, the US Army tried very hard to persuade the British to purchase the Abrams tank. It was well known in the British Army that the outdated Challenger tank needed to be replaced. The decision to purchase had been elevated to the Prime Minister's office. Prime Minister Thatcher was invited to the US Embassy for a closed-door briefing on the Abrams tank and the process of the British purchasing the tank. The briefing team included Ambassador Price, a Major General from the US Army, me, and Prime Minister Thatcher. After a quick twenty-minute slide show on the Abrams, Prime Minister Thatcher turned to the three of us and said, "Gentlemen, I have no doubt that the Abrams is a fine tank, but we must make our own." We knew that an experienced politician had made a difficult political decision.

The statement was a final decision, and shortly thereafter, the British began developing and fielding the Challenger II tank. While a very capable tank that performed quite well during the Gulf War, it lacked some of the capabilities of the Abrams M2 that was fielded during that conflict.

### *Lectures at the Ministry of Defence*

Between 1987 and 1990, twice a year, I was asked to provide an overview of the US military at a civil servant seminar for those working in the UK's Ministry of Defence. On one occasion, there were multiple questions about our Navy. One very distinguished-looking gentleman asked about the size of the US Navy in a manner that appeared to me that he regretted the fact that England had lost this particular colony about 150 years ago.

After a number of less pertinent questions, he raised his voice and said, "Do I understand that your Navy has women fighter pilots?" I was annoyed by this person's persistent questions and responded, "Sir, you are correct. In fact, we have more women fighter pilots in our Navy than your Navy has fighter pilots." At that time, the number of Navy fighter pilots in the British Navy was quite low, so my response, while not based upon facts, was likely correct. This exchange ended my lecture invitations, and I was not invited back.

# Chapter 19: The Joint Staff the Second Time Around

I reported to the J5 section, Joint Chiefs of Staff, two days prior to the Iraqi invasion of Kuwait. The J5 was organized into various regional and functional areas of responsibility. I was assigned to the Division responsible for all European Nations and Russia. There were four branches in the European Division, each headed by an O6 from all four services. Three branches were responsible for geographic areas, and one for NATO members exclusively.

Saddam Hussein's invasion of Kuwait on August 2 required a major shift in emphasis for the European Division. The new focus was to solicit support from these National partners for operations in the Gulf. The following vignette illustrates the shift in emphasis since the end of the Cold War.

While the US moved massive amounts of men and material to Saudi Arabia, it also deployed all available Patriot anti-missile defensive systems to protect US forces deployed to Saudi Arabia. At the same time, the Allied coalition was conducting air strikes against Iraqi forces from bases in Turkey. As Iraqi SCUDS, a medium-range ballistic missile, began to fall in Israel and on US bases in Saudi, the Turks asked for protection from SCUDS that might be launched against them. We responded that all our Patriot batteries were committed, and we could not deploy any to Turkey. The Germans immediately responded that, as a NATO partner, German Patriot batteries could be deployed to Turkey with C5 airlift support from us. However, all our C5 missions were committed to supporting forces in Saudi Arabia. We could lease Russian aircraft to transport the German Patriots to Turkey. I would love to have been at Tbilisi airport when Bundeswehr Patriot batteries rolled out the back of Russian Antonov AN-124s.

Until the launch of ground offensive operations, coordination amongst our European allies was a monumental task we undertook enthusiastically. While the Middle East Division was focused on the preparation for ground offensive operations and strengthening the coalition, European Division officers pulled back-to-back shifts in the National Military Command Center's (NMCC) Crisis Action Team (CAT). The success of the 100-hour war reduced anxiety across the Joint Staff but did little to reduce the European Division's workload.

One of the more humorous events involved my sister, Jan, who was in DC for a conference and stopped by the Pentagon to visit. After escorting her to my office, I received a phone call from our attaché in Tokyo on the secure line. I had a spirited conversation with the attaché about Japanese support for military operations in the Gulf and how much support the Japanese might provide. When I suggested that $24 million would be a good start, out of the corner of my eye, I saw Jan sit up very straight and give me a look of surprise. After concluding my conversation, I reminded Jan that anything she heard in the office had to stay there. She grinned and said, "Well, for $24 million, I think I can keep it quiet." It became an inside joke between the two of us.

# Chapter 20: Hennessey, We Have a Problem

In August 1990, while serving on the Joint Staff in the Pentagon, I received a call to come to the Chairman's office. At this time, General Colin Powell was Chairman of the Joint Chiefs of Staff. I had met General Powell two years earlier when he was the Army Forces Command (FORSCOM) Commander in Atlanta, Georgia.

When I entered his office, the first thing he said was,

"Colonel Hennessey, we have a problem."

He then told me that he had just learned that Secretary of State George Schultz and Russian Foreign Secretary Shevardnadze had made an agreement that he was not sure could be satisfied. That agreement was that the US and Russia would each provide an Intercontinental Ballistic Missile (ICBM) eliminated in SALT II to a Russian artist preparing a sculpture for the United Nations Peace Garden. The SALT II agreement and missile systems eliminated the US Minuteman III and the Russian RS18.

I said, "Yes, Sir, I can see the problem. We don't have any Minuteman III ICBMs left to give the Russian sculptor. Under the Strategic Arms Limitation Treaty II (SALT II) agreement, we have destroyed all of ours. So obviously, the Russians still have some to give away."

General Powell said, "You are right and will help me solve this problem. Let me know when you have some recommendations."

I returned to my office, called my section chiefs, and outlined our challenge. After they repeated my statement that we had destroyed all the Minuteman III ICBMs, I asked them where we might find some still in one piece or how a complete one could be assembled from parts.

After a week of investigating all the possible options for providing a Minuteman III ICBM, we could only find fully authentic fiberglass training model replicas in the Department of Defense. Unfortunately, a genuine US Minuteman III was required because the Russian sculptor would cut them up. So then, one of the officers suggested we look in the Air and Space Museum. According to him, there was a display of both a Minuteman III and a Russian RS18 in the museum. Apparently, at the culmination of the SALT II agreement, the US and Russia each donated an ICBM to the Air and Space Museum.

Hoping that the Minuteman III on display was not a fiberglass mockup, we contacted the Air and Space Museum. We found that it was a real ICBM, not a fiberglass replica. Negotiations were left to DOD lawyers as to how the actual Minuteman III missile might be replaced with an entirely realistic training model replica.

I wish I had been there for the transfer because it was a midnight operation that replaced the real Minuteman III with a fiberglass replica that was then transported to the location of the sculptor. A few years later, I visited the United Nations and saw the result of the sculptor's work.

While I am no art critic, the sculpture could not be uglier, unexciting, and a total waste of two complete ICBMs. The piece is titled "Good Destroys Evil" and depicts a figure supposedly of St George slaying the dragon. Unfortunately, that dragon comprises fragments of a US Minuteman III and a Russian RS18.

So, should you ever visit the Air and Space Museum in downtown Washington, DC, you now know the real story behind the display of a US and a Russian ICBM. Of the two missiles displayed, only one is real.

# Chapter 21: My Taiwan Experience

After my retirement from the Army, I was a research professor at the Institute of Public Policy (TIPP), now the Schar School of Policy and Government, at George Mason University. TIPP has just won a contract to assist the Taiwanese government in what was euphemistically termed a "right-sizing" initiative. As background, President Chiang Kai Shak moved the national government to Taiwan in 1949. As an island state within the larger China, Taiwan already had its own provincial government. Thus, for the past fifty-plus years, Taiwan had two levels of government. The contract called for a lecture series for civil servants throughout the major government centers in Taiwan. The Dean asked me if I would be interested in the assignment, and I agreed to accept. After preparing my lectures and submitting them to the Taiwanese government for translation and publishing, I left Dulles Airport for a long trip to Taiwan.

Upon my arrival, I was met by Ms. Wang, my guide and interpreter, for the next two weeks. She was a graduate student studying English at National Taiwan University (NTU) and was fluent in English and Mandarin. The Taiwanese I met were incredibly hospitable, and I had some of the best food. One of the unique features of Taiwanese dining, at least to me, was the "hot pot." I have seen this in a very rudimentary table and in some of the more sophisticated restaurants. The table is usually round and has an open burner in the middle into which a pot of flavored broth is placed. Any number of vegetables, meats, and spices are then cooked in the pot and shared with the diners at the table.

I delivered twelve lectures on governmental organizational models, particularly how Taiwan might flatten its governmental structure. In each, the question-and-answer periods were both energetic and informational. In one instance, an elderly gentleman rose with a question. Since the questions were always in Mandarin, my interpreter would translate the question for me in the earpiece I wore.

When I answered the question, she would provide my response in Mandarin. When the gentleman asked his question, I looked into the control booth expecting a translation from my interpreter. After a hesitant "Umm." Ms. Wang said, "I haven't a clue what he just asked." I asked her to have the gentleman repeat his question, and fortunately, she understood the second time and translated for me. It is strange to stand on stage in front of 50-60 government officials and have your interpreter say, "Um, I haven't a clue response."

The Taiwanese government wanted me to experience as much culture as possible while traveling. On one visit to a park a couple of hours from Taipei, Ms. Wang arranged for a picnic lunch to be picked up on the way. She asked if I liked chicken fingers. I said I did and expected them to be part of the lunch. When it came time to open the various packages for lunch, she handed me a container. Expecting the Taiwanese equivalent of American chicken fingers, I was surprised to find chicken feet in the red sauce instead. To stifle my surprise, I asked Ms. Wang if she wanted "chicken fingers." She replied in no uncertain terms, "I could never eat those things." The "chicken fingers" were left uneaten by the two of us.

After twelve lectures and visits to many Taiwanese cultural locations, including a one-day visit to an amazing hot springs resort, it was time for me to return to the US. The contract called for the Taiwanese government to pay for my transportation to and from Taiwan and a per diem amount for each day of the trip. Since my office had arranged for the travel, the amount of funds due to my organization included the airfare and the per diem. Once we agreed on the final amount, I received the payment in an 18-inch stack of Taiwanese dollars. I was told my conversion rate would be better if I converted the Taiwanese dollars to US dollars before leaving Taiwan. I was surprised that the stack of Taiwanese dollars ended up being a twelve-inch stack of fifty-and-one-hundred-dollar bills amounting to over $20,000 US dollars. I could hardly stuff the money into my jacket and backpack.

The paperwork provided by the Taiwanese government and the contract satisfied the customs officials at Dulles when I declared I had more than $10,000 in cash on me. My arrival on a Saturday made it impossible to deliver the funds to the University finance office that would open on Monday.

I thoroughly enjoyed my visit to Taiwan and have great respect for the Taiwanese. Not long after my return to the States, Ms. Wang sent me a CD with pictures of the many places I visited and historical and cultural locations I did not have time to visit. Sometimes you get to do things you never imagined you would, and the job is more pleasure than work.

# Chapter 22: Dissertation Research Adventures

In 1994, I was in the process of finishing my doctorate at George Mason University. To complete the program, I had to submit a dissertation that a university committee approved. After approving my proposed hypothesis and research agenda, I began the data collection portion. My data collection included surveys, interviews, and questionnaires administered in two federal agencies: the Defence Contract Management Command (DCMC) and the Veterans Benefits Administration (VBA). I recognized that I had to travel to many parts of the country to reach both DCMC and VBA offices in the same city. I sought a meeting with the Commander, DCMC, and outlined my work and how it might benefit the organization. He agreed to fund my travel as long as I shared the results with him.

At the same time, Vice President Al Gore was promoting the "Hammer Award." The Hammer Awards were Vice President Gore's special recognition for teams of federal workers who made important contributions to reinventing a piece of the United States Government. The goals of that program were: Putting Customers First, Cutting Red Tape, Empowering Employees, and Getting Back to Basics. The program centered around the administration's effort to "reinvent government." I hypothesized that organizational culture and leadership are essential elements of organizational success, which fit the program goals. I received a letter from Vice President Gore emphasizing the importance of my research. I only used this letter once after being discreetly advised that using the Vice President's encouragement letter made me a "government guy."

I was fortunate to be able to use the Price Waterhouse assessment tool and worked with advisors to craft interview questions that were pertinent to my research. The schedule of visits to VBA and DCMC locations was put together. I visited the following cities: New York (three times), Boston, Atlanta, Milwaukee, Los Angeles, and San Juan, Puerto Rico. The selection process was easy in that each VBA and DCMC office in each city had either received a Hammer Award or was being considered for one.

I started in New York City and visited the VBA office led by Jim Thompson. When I first saw their building, it was a bit of a déjà vu. The front of the building had a covered walkway around the front of the building to protect those on the sidewalk from the falling brick façade. I was later told that the concertina wire on the roof was to keep the homeless from going onto the roof. Some homeless had recently gone on the roof of the covered walkway and started a fire to keep warm. The plywood roof quickly caught fire, and the concertina barbed wire was to discourage future visitors. It looked like the old downtown Saigon hotel with barricades and barbed wire. The VBA office on the eighth floor was accessed by an elevator that also serviced the methadone clinic for drug abusers on the ninth floor.

My second visit to New York City found me in a totally different VBA office. Jim Thompson had his auditor go back through their GSA payment schedule. They found they had been overpaying GSA for the building lease for many years. Government regulations allowed agencies to recoup overpayments, allowing this VBA office to move to Seventh Avenue in a new building. Jim Thompson also began a program to verify the need for particular reports. At the time, the Veterans Administration required VBA offices to submit over a hundred monthly reports. Many of which most suspected were never read. He started with the report of minutes between a veteran signing in and being seen by a counselor. As all the office members were trained as counselors, as soon as a veteran signed in, he or she was seen. His report was always zero minutes. The suspicion that the reports were seldom read was confirmed when no one questioned the zero minutes report for a year. At the end of the year, Jim Thompson's office stopped sending that report, and again there was no response. I understand that he did this for a number of other reports.

Veterans seeking assistance at a VBA office have two choices regarding how they can receive that assistance. They can call the office and talk to a counselor, or they can visit the office and talk to a counselor. Two case scenarios indicate how veterans in one area trust the VBA counselors and how they do not trust them in another. In Milwaukee, the VBA office has a large, easily accessible parking lot within two miles of three interstate highways. Veterans in the area can then easily access the VBA office. In Los Angeles, the VBA office is on Wilshire Boulevard and has no parking lot. Parking is difficult, as is traffic along this busiest part of Los Angeles. It makes traveling to the VBA office very difficult. So, where do veterans travel to the VBA office, and where do they call in? Exactly the opposite of what you might expect. In Los Angeles, they want to talk face-to-face with the counselor. In Milwaukee, they call in to talk with a counselor. It was all a matter of trust. In Los Angeles, the VBA counselors were only partially trusted, while veterans had complete trust in their counselors in Milwaukee.

# Chapter 23: Teaching Public Administration on Capitol Hill

In early 2004, I taught a senior-level course in Public Administration at George Mason University. As part of the course, I secured the support of two Virginia Members of Congress to sponsor a "Day on the Hill" for the students.

I provided a list of students, and the staff of Representative Jim Moran arranged entry for the students and meeting space for the class. My coordination with other staff included senior House and Senate Armed Services Committee and the Congressional Budget Office staff. Often, we would be welcomed by either Representative Tom Davis or Representative Jim Moran. Interestingly, Davis, a Republican, and Moran, a Democratic, were close friends and worked well in the House of Representatives.

The students were on their own to arrive at the Capitol on time. On the other hand, I would leave enough time to swing by Dunkin Donuts and pick up my order of ten dozen donuts. After finding a parking place close to the Capitol, I loaded my class materials and donuts on a cart and walked to the House entrance. Within a year, I had the opportunity to meet many of the Capitol Police. Leaving a dozen donuts with the crew at the entrance made me a memorable character.

The morning was spent on the House side with presentations and discussions with staff members from the various House committees.

The professionalism of each staff member struck us, but we also noticed something different. That difference was that some committee staff used the opportunity to have new staff gain experience in briefing and discussing committee issues. Others were senior staff members, and their confidence in their briefing was quite apparent. The takeaway for most students was that the committee's senior staff were subject matter experts. A House Member's reliance on those committee staff members was clear. That contrasted with the House Member's office staff. While the Chief of Staff might be a seasoned veteran, most office staff were on the job for less than a year, and many were interns.

After lunch in the House cafeteria, we moved to the Senate side of the Capitol, where Senator John Warner hosted the group. What is most striking about moving from the House side of the Capitol building to the Senate side is the décor and decorum. The hearing rooms where we met were much more decorative, with wood paneling and ornate light fixtures. The contrast in service was also striking. In the House, we provided our own donuts, and coffee was served from disposable containers in paper cups. On the Senate side, coffee was served in silver coffee service, and each student had a porcelain coffee cup. We were also provided with cookies and pastries on silver platters. The difference was striking, to say the least.

Senator John Warner must have had a soft spot in his heart for the George Mason students because he often spent at least an hour with the class. Those sessions were, both for the students and for me, some of the most insightful observations of the political process we had ever heard.

A side note on Senator Warner. In 2005, he was invited to be the Commencement Speaker at George Mason. One of my responsibilities was to line up the platform party in the long hallway at the end of the Patriot Center (now Eagle Bank Arena). As we waited to process, a young lady burst through an adjoining door to the ladies' room across the hallway. She was as green as her gown and didn't reach the bathroom. She threw up as she passed Senator Warner and hit his shoes on her way. As only a Southern gentleman would, Senator Warner helped her to the ladies' room and wiped off his shoes with his handkerchief. His only comment was, "Seems that young lady celebrated a little too much last night."

Our "Day on the Hill" was long, and both I and the students were exhausted by the end of the day. Nonetheless, every student said the educational experience was one of the best they had ever had in a class at Mason. My next two class meetings were spent reviewing what they had learned on Capitol Hill and contrasting that with their assigned readings. Unsurprisingly, students found inconsistencies and conflicts between what they had heard and experienced and what they read. For me, that is the ultimate teaching moment.

# Chapter 24: Unexpected Talent

In 1996, the Institute of Public Policy (TIPP) at George Mason University competed for and won a bid to assist the Internal Revenue Service (IRS) modernize its processing system. A number of faculty members of TIPP were to be involved in the contract. I was included in the group, and we planned how to approach the various tasks required to assist the IRS effort.

First, among the tasks we identified was to travel to various IRS processing centers and observe the current processing system. Among those we were to visit was a major center in Kansas City, Missouri. I volunteered to set up the arrangements for the visit, including renting a car for our use.

During my previous career in the US Army, I was required to take what is euphemistically termed "counterterrorism driving." During that training, we learned how to avoid being trapped on highways and roads, look ahead for escape routes, and generally avoid being a casualty while driving. I also learned which vehicles were the safest to drive. The car I rented for our trip to Kansas City was a Volvo 560, one of the safest cars at the time.

Our airline trip to Kansas City airport was uneventful, and we picked up the car at the rental counter. Because I made the reservation, I was the designated driver. After loading our bags and confirming our destination, we began the twelve-mile journey to the processing center. This route required that we travel on the interstate highway that went along the east, south, and west sides of Kansas City. Initially, the traffic was light and more congested as we approached our exit.

Suddenly, about a half mile ahead, a long flatbed truck with telephone pole-sized logs began to lose the load and spill the logs across the highway. Panicked drivers ahead of us and on all three lanes began frantically dodging the still-moving logs. We could hear the squeal of brakes, the crashing of the logs, and the metal crunches as cars sideswiped or crashed into each other. There were loud exclamations of concern by the other passengers, especially when I drove off the highway and onto the median. Traveling at 60 miles an hour on the median was something other than what they had expected.

Instinctively I had been looking for escape routes should, for any reason, the roadway be blocked. I took the escape route I had already identified when it was blocked. We traveled the quarter mile beyond the pileup of vehicles and logs along the median and then back onto the highway. My three passengers breathed a sigh of relief, and one asked, "What the hell just happened?" I then told them about the driving course I had taken while on active duty and how I had learned to avoid accidents like that.

The three faculty members were intrigued by my driving course and wanted to learn more about it. After telling them about learning how to stop quickly and safely at 90+ miles an hour, turn around using the brakes and accelerator, and ram a roadblock vehicle in the right place, I also told them about the downside of the experience.

Having spent the better part of three days speeding around race tracks at high speeds and performing other vehicle maneuvers, I was now on my way home on the Capital Beltway. I found that all the cars and trucks on the Beltway were moving so slowly, and I could not understand why. Then I glanced at my speedometer and found to my chagrin, that I was cruising along at 90 miles an hour! No wonder everyone seemed to be going so much slower. As I slowed to a more sedate 65 miles an hour in the right lane, a state police vehicle pulled alongside me in the center lane. I fully expected to be pulled over and issued a citation for speeding. Then, much to my surprise and that of the police officer, a vehicle passed him, going at least 100 miles an hour in the left lane. The police officer took off after him, and I stayed with the traffic and the speed limit all the way home.

From then on, my colleagues at TIPP called me the best driver they ever had and regaled others with their stories of how Hennessey had saved them on a trip. I was also the designated driver whenever we traveled together.

# Chapter 25: Meeting Amazing People

While working at George Mason University as a research assistant professor, research was the favorite part of my academic activity. During that research, I had the occasion to meet some amazing people. None was more amazing than Noman M. Cole, Jr.

I first met Noman at the 1996 Northern Virginia Leadership Conference at George Mason. Among his presentations, he described how Virginia forced Maryland and the District of Columbia to implement the 1972 Clean Water Act fully.

Appointed as Chair of the State Water Control Board by the first elected Republican governor in Virginia since the Civil War, Noman was an outspoken critic of regional failures to control the flow of raw sewage into the Potomac River. As a senior in high school in Alexandria, Virginia, in 1960, I remember watching parts of the Potomac River burn at night—the amount of methane released by the raw sewage burned off as the river swept it downstream.

Noman, in addition to being a great engineer, was also a shrewd politician. With the Governor of Virginia's approval, he invited the Mayor of DC and the governor of Maryland to a flyover of the Potomac River. The four-foot-wide pipe discharging raw sewage into the Potomac was clearly visible just below the Kennedy Center. A federal lawsuit soon followed, and the District of Columbia and the state of Maryland instituted the necessary changes in processing wastewater.

# Fairy Tales and War Stories

In 1986 the nuclear power plant in Chornobyl exploded, and efforts to contain the radiation emitted by the blast required a significant international effort. Noman served on the international group that developed the containment strategy for the power plant. Many credit Noman with developing the containment dome that now encases the reactor buildings in the power plant. Analysis of the cause of the disaster identified both poor design and poor procedures. Noman spent considerable time with Russian engineers to correct the procedures in other plants to avoid another accident.

Tragically, this gifted engineer, dedicated public servant, and champion for clear water died in a skiing accident in the Fall of 1997. Governor Linwood Holton, who appointed Noman to the Water Control Board, eulogized Noman as a dedicated public servant.

After my appointment as the University Chief of Staff, one of my responsibilities was to greet important visitors on behalf of the President. Not long after the introduction of US forces into Afghanistan, President Hamid Karzai came to campus to address a gathering of Afghans living in Northern Virginia. Little did we realize that so many Afghans lived in the area. As I made my way from my office to the concert hall where the assembly would be held, I marveled at the number of cars and people arriving.

I met with the diplomatic security detail assigned to President Karsai and waited for his motorcade. I greeted him at the entrance to the concert hall and assured him that we had encouraged all the students, staff, and faculty with any Afghan connections to join him. He told me that he appreciated our hospitality and the kindness that we had shown to all his staff. His fluent English and pertinent questions about the university impressed me. I did not stay for his address to the 5000+ gathered to hear him but thought to myself as I returned to my office that he seemed an extremely good example of the type of political leader the United States finds easy to work with.

# Chapter 26: Working with Members of Congress

In 1995, The Institute of Public Policy (TIPP), where I was a faculty member, was approached by the Congressional Institute for the Future (CIF) to examine a possible partnership. CIF was founded in 1979 by Senators Al Gore (D) and John Heinz (R). Its purpose was to provide insight into issues beyond the current legislative horizon to members of Congress. Those were the days when Members of Congress worked together.

A partnership between TIPP and CIF was hammered out. Part of the agreement was that TIPP would provide the Executive Director for CIF, and the staff at CIF would have access through the Executive Director to the academic assets of the University. The Dean of TIPP asked me to take the job, and I spent the next four years either in the offices on Capitol Hill or in a classroom teaching at George Mason. I approached this job like any new unit in the Army I joined. I asked the five staff members how they accomplished the CIF mission, what they needed from me as the Executive Director, and how I might contribute to their success. I believe they knew I was not there to tell them how to do their job but rather to improve CIF's work and improve their outreach to Congress.

At CIF, we facilitated our mission through briefings and dinners for Members of Congress with notable experts in many fields. One such dinner held in a Senate hearing room highlighted the work of Andy Grove, the first President of Intel. Congressional attendees included Senator Diane Feinstein of California and senior staff from the Senate and House. This was one of the more popular events, and I had the uncomfortable task of telling more than a few Members that they were not invited.

The dinner topic was the growth of technology in many aspects of everyday life. In particular, Grove emphasized how transformative technology was in education and research. This led to a lengthy discussion of how the internet will change how we do almost everything in the future.

During this conversation, Senator Feinstein began discussing the role of the internet in exposing children to pornography and violence. It was clear from the beginning that she was deeply concerned about the issue and offered some thoughts about how Congress might be involved in any effort to limit the effects of the internet.

Andy Grove then made the point that at sixteen years of age, teenagers are often given the keys to a four-thousand-pound automobile and expected to operate it safely. He said, "Our expectation is based upon the training and supervised experience the teenager has received at home and school. So, we should provide a commensurate level of training and experience to any child before they are permitted unfettered access to a computer." I cannot be sure that Senator Feinstein accepted the analogy provided by Dr. Grove, but it gave a number of senior staff a few good chuckles.

Later that year, we invited a group of researchers from the Massachusetts Institute of Technology (MIT) to demonstrate their "intelligent glasses." These glasses had multiple technologies embedded in them. First among these was facial recognition software. That software was paired with data sets that allowed the wearer to see an individual face to face, have the facial recognition software identify him or her, and then pull up relevant information about that individual and display it on the inside of the glasses.

You cannot imagine the excitement these "intelligent glasses" caused among the congressmen and congresswomen. They could imagine being able to identify constituents by name, know their backgrounds, and, more importantly, their donation status. At that moment, the glasses were clunky and looked more like those worn by Buddy Holly than anything stylish.

The MIT folks were excited by the prospect of receiving additional funding to expand their research. I often wonder how many Members of Congress are now wearing some later generation of these original "intelligent glasses."

On another occasion, we hosted a session with British developmental biologist Ian Wilmut, who, with colleagues from the Roslin Institute near Edinburgh, Scotland, cloned Dolly, the first clone of an adult mammal. This was big news, and the topic was hot on everyone's mind. Unfortunately, the exquisitely intricate explanation provided by Dr. Wilmut went so far over the head of most attendees that they were at a loss to ask any intelligent questions. The obvious implications for human cloning were apparent; some in attendance expressed their concerns that this might not be a great advance in biological engineering.

# Chapter 27: A 9/11 Memoir

For many of us, 9/11 changed how we do business and look at the world. So too, was it a major change in how we operated at George Mason University. As the University Chief of Staff, I was in the School of Education Dean's office that morning when a secretary came in and said that a plane had hit one of the buildings in New York City. It was not long until we learned the full extent of the terrorist attacks. And from that moment, how we perceived the world and responded to emergencies changed.

On September 11, 2001, there were forty-one higher education teaching locations in the Greater Washington metropolitan area. Most were small instructional locations for out-of-state schools. Still, those with residential campuses included Northern Virginia Community College (NOVA), George Mason, Maryland, George Washington, Georgetown, and American and Catholic universities. Thanks to our rapid news cycle, more than 200,000 full-time and part-time college students experienced first-hand the terrorist attack on America. Unfortunately, with only one exception, those same students went to their dormitories or homes and watched the attacks repeatedly on television. Within the first two hours after the attack, faculty in an academic unit of George Mason, the Institute for Conflict Analysis and Resolution, who had experience responding to terrorist attacks, provided valuable advice. Their response was unanimous, "Don't close. Provide a place for students, staff, and faculty to have some semblance of normality."

# Fairy Tales and War Stories

Due to the decision to remain open, George Mason was the only school in the Washington Metropolitan area that did not close. One of the more challenging conversations I had that morning was with our Vice President for the Arlington campus, only a mile from the now-smoking Pentagon. He called me at about 9:30 am and said they could see the smoke from the Pentagon and that he would close the campus. I told him that he would not close and that the only instructions he would give staff, faculty, and students were that classes were canceled, but the campus was open. Twice he asked, "You mean classes are canceled, and the campus is closed, right?" The final time I said very slowly, "Listen to me. Classes are canceled on the Arlington campus, but the campus remains open. Do you understand?"

Earlier, Arlington County authorities and VDOT (Virginia Department of Transportation) had requested that we not hold classes out of concern that it would add to the traffic already building in the county. In addition to the advice from our faculty, I knew we had to keep the campus open because many could not or would not want to leave.

Meanwhile, the Provost instructed faculty on the Fairfax and Prince William campuses that unless they had to be away, they were to hold class and provide an opportunity for students to deal with their responses to the attacks. The President of George Mason directed all the senior administrators to walk across campus and be visible to students, staff, and faculty. The university counseling center recruited student facilitators, experienced staff, and faculty to organize "counseling corners" wherever they could. These were then positioned all over campus as places where students, staff, and faculty gathered and shared their concerns and responses to the events of the day. Early in the afternoon, the President held a brief gathering of students, staff, and faculty outside the largest academic building to memorialize those who had lost their lives and remind everyone that the most important thing that could be done in the short term was to continue to succeed as students, staff and faculty. He reminded everyone that we had counseling corners all over campus and that faculty would continue to teach their classes.

Separately, the President and the Provost asked the faculty to give special attention to those affected directly by the attacks. With so many Northern Virginia families connected to the military, we knew the attack would directly impact many in the Pentagon.

At 7:20 that evening, I was scheduled to teach a graduate class in Public Administration. When I arrived at 7:00, I had no idea how many students would show up because so many of my students were working professionals, many with close connections to the Pentagon and the Department of Defense. To my surprise, there were very few absences. I started the class by making some remarks about the historic nature of the day, how it would be a lot like our parents and grandparents' memories of the attack on Pearl Harbor, and that, as public administration scholars, we needed to appreciate the significance of what had happened and how we responded to it.

During our extended discussions, two students shared their personal experiences that day. One young woman described standing at one of the Pentagon bus stops when American Airlines flight 77 crashed into her office on the Pentagon's southwest side. I learned later that it was over three days before she learned exactly what had happened to her office mates. Unfortunately, most people she worked with were either killed or injured.

Shortly after class started, another student came in a little late, apologizing for the smell he had brought with him. As a District of Columbia Fire Department fire captain, his crew's first response was to the White House. When they were released from that response, the crew was sent to the Pentagon to help fight the fire started by American Flight 77 when it struck the Pentagon. He and his crew were the firefighters on television atop the Pentagon, attempting to contain the fire. The student told us that when the Pentagon was built in 1941, the roof was insulated with fourteen inches of horse hair. That's what was smoldering through the roof! Our fire captain student had taken three showers, but the smell remained. The smell also pervaded Arlington County for the next few days.

The next three hours of class were some of the most intense sharing of how local government was operating in crisis that I had experienced in more than twenty years in graduate courses. More than anything else, class discussions struck me, led almost exclusively by the students. It was a teaching moment that few faculty members ever had. I should not have been surprised because this class was part of the graduate Masters of Public Administration program, and we focused on local government organization and process improvement. Most of my students either worked in local or federal governments or, through their experience, had unique insights into the processes we saw firsthand during the entire day. Many of the students were familiar with the emergency response plans in Fairfax, Prince William, and Arlington counties. They described how the agencies backed up each other in this instance. The three counties (Arlington, Fairfax, and Prince William) in Northern Virginia share long boundaries and many similarities. Arlington County's fire and EMS capabilities were committed to the Pentagon. Fairfax County police, fire, and EMS responded to all Arlington County emergency calls on 9/11. Prince William County provided backup for Fairfax County when its police, fire, and EMS services were stretched thin.

While most of us would probably not notice the difference in the markings of a police car, fire truck, or ambulance responding to our emergency, most Arlington residents on 9/11 received responses from Fairfax County police, fire, and EMS. So, too did some Fairfax residents see responses from Prince William County police, fire, and EMS.

Some criticized the leadership of George Mason University for not closing that day. The many who recognized that remaining open was the best course of action quickly drowned out those voices. While our Institute for Conflict Analysis and Resolution faculty was instrumental in our decision to remain open, I was singled out as the most visible advocate. My reward for that action was also being in charge of all emergency preparation and responses for the university. Just another example of no "good deed" goes unpunished.

# Chapter 28: "I Know Something About the Law"

From 1999 until 2012, I served as the George Mason University Chief of Staff. One of my responsibilities was the liaison between the Board of Visitors and the University. The Board of Visitors in the Commonwealth of Virginia is the governing board for each public institution. Each school has a different number of Visitors, a title derived from Thomas Jefferson's directive that a group of "distinguished visitors would determine the conduct and efficiency of the university." While applied originally to the University of Virginia, it has been applied to all public state colleges and universities. All visitors are appointed by the Governor of Virginia and serve staggered terms. As single-term governors, each Virginia governor could rarely appoint more than four visitors to the George Mason Board.

George Mason University had a sixteen-member Board of Visitors chaired by the "rector" elected by the membership. I enjoyed working with former United States Attorney General Edwin Meese for my first six years. Mr. Meese's leadership style was very participative, and he insisted that each board member contribute during deliberations.

During an executive session, when University Counsel briefed the board on an issue likely to end up in court, one Visitor monopolized the conversation. Although not a lawyer, this Visitor droned on and on about how this would damage the reputation of the university and might also cause significant hardship if the court found the university liable. He tried to bring up historical examples of similar events that damaged the schools' reputations.

All the time the Visitor gives his doom and gloom script, Mr. Meese is watching him and not saying a word. Other board members are now watching Mr. Meese to see if he has any response to the other visitors' ramblings. When the vociferous visitor appears finished with his speech, Mr. Meese calmly says, "Thank you for your input, Visitor X, but I think I know a bit about the law." He then turned to the University Counsel and asked him to complete his presentation.

The visitor that had dominated the conversation for so long suddenly realized whom he was lecturing on issues of law. His face paled, and he stammered some excuse for his lengthy and utterly useless contribution. The University Counsel then made a strong recommendation approved by the Board, and Mr. Meese congratulated the University Counsel on the presentation and the well-thought-out recommendation. The recommendation was that the case be brought to trial and that the university not agree to a settlement.

Unfortunately for me, I was designated as the University representative for the case, and along with the University Counsel, I had to appear in the Federal Court Judge's chambers and explain why the case could not be settled out of court. My explanation was sufficient to bring the case to trial. The good news was that the University prevailed, and the plaintiff paid attorney fees and court costs.

# Chapter 29: What is a Legislative Liaison?

One of the roles of the University Chief of Staff at George Mason University was university liaison to the General Assembly of Virginia. Fortunately or unfortunately, the General Assembly meets for 90 days one year and 45 days the next. The schedule for legislators and those working with the General Assembly is compressed during those sessions. During those sessions, I was either on the road early enroute to Richmond or stayed overnight. Committee meetings sometimes started at 7:00 am, so an early start was important.

The most important role of the university liaison was to promote the general higher education budget and university-specific amendments to the biannual budget. I was extremely fortunate for two reasons. One, the House Appropriations Committee chairman, was a delegate from Fairfax who had been a University Board of Visitors member. Second, the Senate Finance Committee Chair was from Prince William County and a strong supporter of our growing campus there. Both had a keen understanding of the university's needs. While other university liaisons had to go around to various delegate and senate offices to obtain support for their amendments, I only had to leave mine on the desk of the two Chairmen.

Each liaison reviewed pending legislation and referred specific higher education legislation to appropriate offices at the university. I was no exception and often found the insight that others had invaluable in addressing the legislation's effects on the university. On one occasion, a legislator committed to helping veterans proposed legislation allowing a veteran's child to receive tuition assistance based on the veteran's disability rating from the Veterans Administration. Unfortunately, the way the legislation was written, any veteran's child from any state would benefit. I understood his intent and worked with him to ensure that this important piece of legislation applied only to residents of Virginia.

On multiple occasions, legislation would be offered to allow students to have and carry weapons on campus. While I firmly support the second amendment, I also know the limitations that must be applied to safeguard a campus of young adults. When a committee meeting was held, and this legislation was on the agenda, I made it a point to let the sponsor know that I would object to the legislation. When those opposed to the legislation were allowed to speak, I would ask three questions and ask anyone who answered yes to raise their hand. I would first ask, *"How many of you have been in a gunfight?"* And raise my hand. *"How many of you have shot someone in a gunfight?"* And I would keep my hand raised. *"How many of you have been shot in a gunfight?"* And I would keep my hand raised. My comments were then preceded by, "Since I am the only one with my hand still raised, let me tell you why this legislation is not a good idea for a college campus. Quick explanations ranging from how college-age drinking and weapons don't mix well to the difficulty in identifying the good and bad guys in a gunfight convinced most legislators to drop or table the bills.

Most trips to and from Richmond could not have been more uneventful. Because the General Assembly began meeting in January, even the short session guaranteed some difficult weather might happen. One such bad weather event found me attempting to leave Richmond at 4:00 pm. It had been snowing for a while, and Interstate 95 had slowed to a crawl. As I approached the outskirts of Richmond, traffic began to stop and go with more stops than go. I looked at my fuel gauge and realized I needed to get some gas quickly. Then traffic stopped almost completely, and I found my bladder began to fill as quickly as my fuel dropped. After an agonizing thirty minutes with my fuel gauge on dead empty and my back teeth about to float, I could exit I-95 and get to a gas station. I was one of many with this idea; the line at the gas pumps was almost as long as the line at the men's room. I sympathized with the many ladies waiting in line at the ladies' room but hurried to fill up and get back on the road. A trip that normally took ninety minutes was stretched to three hours. Such is the weather in Virginia.

# Chapter 30: Nobel Laureate in the Virginia General Assembly

In 2002, Vernon Smith was awarded the Nobel Prize for Economics. At that time, he was a faculty member in the Economics Department at George Mason University. He joined James Buchanan, who received the same award in 1986 as the second Nobel Laureate at George Mason.

Each year at the beginning of the legislative session, the Governor of Virginia delivers a "State of State" speech to the General Assembly that convenes each January. Vernon received his Nobel Prize on December 8, 2002, and there was great publicity about the event. Later in December 2002, President Alan Merten received a call from Governor Jim Gilmore inviting Vernon Smith to be recognized at this speech. As the University Chief of Staff, Dr. Merten asked me to facilitate Vernon's visit to the Capitol in Richmond for the Governor's speech.

As the University Chief of Staff, I also served as the University Liaison to the Virginia General Assembly. In that job, I knew the Capitol and the behind-the-scenes staff that would make the visit much easier. Vernon and I met briefly the day before the visit and confirmed the timing of the event and our travel plans. Some critics of Virginia politics have said that while Fairfax, where we were located, is only 100 miles from Richmond, it's actually a hundred years apart.

We left in a university car on a chilly, dark sky the morning of the Governor's speech. Fortunately, the forecasted snow did not arrive, and we arrived in Richmond on time. We parked in the reserved space behind the Capitol Building and hurried into the warm vestibule. We were met by a member of the Governor's staff and led to the balcony seating overlooking the House of Delegates chamber.

On the way to Richmond, I had the opportunity to educate Vernon and his wife on the history of the General Assembly and the Office of the Governor. He was quite surprised to learn that the General Assembly of Virginia is the longest continuous national legislative body in modern history. He was further surprised to learn that the Governor's term ended soon after the speech, and he could not be reelected—one of the few states with one-term Governors.

There is little I remember about Governor Gilmore's speech. I remember his introduction of Vernon Smith and his extolling the virtues of his work in experimental economics. He mentioned more than once that George Mason University was home to more Nobel Laureates than any other institution in the Commonwealth of Virginia. The round of applause that followed the Governor's introduction was thunderous. After the speech, many delegates and senators joined us in the reception and congratulated Vernon.

It's now after 10 pm, and we were back on the road headed north to Fairfax. Fortunately, the snow and the traffic were light, and I could drop Vernon and his wife at their home before midnight. A long day and an interesting one. The opportunity to get to know a Nobel Laureate, watch the elected leadership of Virginia recognize him, and know that the University's reputation and prestige were solidly planted was rewarding.

# Chapter 31: Sex Fest and a Miss Virginia Visit

As University Chief of Staff, one often encounters student initiatives that raise questions. One student initiative from the School of Nursing involved the student group's effort to stage a health fair. The health fair aimed to educate the student body on health issues, from sexually transmitted diseases (STDs) to basic nutrition. They recognized that advertising a health fair would likely not engender much enthusiasm in the student body. So, the enterprising group labeled their health fair a "Sex Fest."

The idea of a Sex Fest being held on the university campus was novel and controversial. The student nurse group capitalized on the issue and marketed the fair aggressively. I soon began receiving concerned inquiries from local legislators and spent much time responding to their questions. It also made the local news in the Washington, DC, area remarkable because the news cycle is so consumed with political news. I received a call from Channel 9 and a request for an interview. The request for the interview included the fair organizer and me and would take place at 5:00 am the next morning. The early interview time was for it to be broadcast on the morning news.

It is important to note that the fair organizer was a very attractive graduate nursing student. The taped interview was made in front of the administration building that morning and hit the TV screens of most Channel 9 viewers by 7:00 am. The reason I know for sure that it was on at 7:00 was that a long-time Army friend called me shortly thereafter. He said, "I just saw you on television with a beautiful young coed discussing sex. How do I get a job like that?" Unfortunately, not all the viewers saw the humor in the interview, and I received more than a few disgruntled phone calls. One phone call was from a very conservative state senator who had criticized the university system for its overly progressive activities in the past.

I assured him that the term "Sex Fest" was a gimmick to get everyone's attention. The fact that he called me about it demonstrated how effective the advertising was. I suggested he attend the fair and let me know if anything was presented that might be offensive. He attended the fair and later confirmed that it was an interesting advertising ploy and was indeed a health fair and accomplished the nursing students' purpose. He noted that the array of aphrodisiacs over the centuries was particularly intriguing.

In 2006, George Mason graduate student Adrianna Sgarlata was crowned Miss Virginia and competed in the Miss America contest that year. Interestingly, she was the third George Mason graduate crowned Miss Virginia in the past five years. She was scheduled for a photo shoot with President Merten on campus in late summer. Just before her arrival, I was in the open area between my office and President Merten's office, talking with a group of four gentlemen who had a scheduled meeting with Dr. Merten. This area had a low wall with glass covering the inside wall around an atrium. Anyone entering the office from the elevator walked around the atrium before entering the Presidential suite. They were also visible to everyone in the vestibule area.

As I talked to the gentlemen, Ms. Sgarlata exited the elevator and walked around the atrium enroute to my office. She was strikingly beautiful with full pageant makeup and a tailored dress. I had my back to the atrium, but the four gentlemen quickly focused on her and stopped talking. I watched four pairs of eyes follow her into the vestibule and approach our group. She and I had met before, and I introduced her to the group and explained the purpose of her visit. I have never seen a group of middle-aged men so tongue-tied. She was a very polished and poised veteran of the pageant circuit as she talked about her preparation for the Miss America contest and how she enjoyed her graduate studies in music at George Mason. She quickly put the four men at ease and, within minutes had them convinced she was the next Miss America.

# Chapter 32: George Mason and the NCAA Final Four

In early 2006, George Mason University's men's basketball team was selected to participate in the NCAA tournament. The basketball team is best known for its progress to the Final Four. In making it to Indianapolis, Mason beat North Carolina, Connecticut, Michigan State, and Wichita State in the Washington, DC, regional.

A UConn alumnus friend recounted seeing the UConn Mason game while in the Atlanta airport. He and a colleague were on a business trip and scheduled a layover in Atlanta to watch the game. The first bar they found was so packed that they could not get a view of the television set. Hurrying along the airport, searching for another bar to watch the game, they saw the bar and heard a loud roar from the television. They both knew that the Washington regional tournament would have a predominantly George Mason crowd. They turned to each other and said, "That doesn't sound good for UConn." If the Verizon Center in Washington, DC, held 25,000, I am sure at least 20,000 were Mason fans.

My wife and I were in Gainesville, Florida, when George Mason beat UConn and left the regional airport when the University of Florida basketball team left for Indianapolis. At the airport, I was wearing my George Mason green logo golf shirt and carrying a George Mason logo carry-on bag. The regional airport in Gainesville is small, with only two gates. While my wife and I were waiting for our flight to load at Gate #1, the University of Florida basketball team headed to Gate #2 for a charter flight to Indianapolis. The look of surprise on Coach Billy Donovan's face when he saw me standing by the entrance to their gate was epic. You could almost imagine what was going through his mind when he saw a George Mason supporter at "his" airport when his team was leaving to play our team.

Just before the Final Four, I was at dinner in Brione's Grille, the local restaurant closest to campus. At the dinner with me were other members of our church's leadership. They were close friends who knew our family, particularly my wife. Much to their surprise, while we were in the middle of dinner, a very attractive blond came to our table, leaned into my ear, and whispered something. I immediately got up and followed her into the bar. I only stayed a few minutes and returned to my table with my church colleagues. They knew the blond was not my wife and did not know who she was. I started to explain what had just happened but liked the tension now apparent around the table. I continued to eat until one of my colleagues said, "OK, Tom, what is the deal with your friend?" I explained that it was Liz Larranaga, Coach Jim Larranaga's wife and that she told me something important I had to see. Jim Larranaga was at the bar with the latest issue of Sports Illustrated, and one of the basketball players was on the front cover. I later learned that the basketball fans in the group soon found the latest copy for their collections.

The leadership of the University, the President, Provost, Senior Vice President, and I met shortly after George Mason qualified for the Final Four. We decided that only three of us could attend the games in Indianapolis. In a flash of altruism, I volunteered to stay behind. I got the promise that I would be there when Mason went to any more NCAA Finals. There was no question the President was going. The only question was which of the three of us would not.

The contrast between the Mason and Florida basketball teams was striking. Liz and Jim Larranaga ensured that each member of the Mason team had a suit, shirt, and tie when they got off the bus at the venue in Indianapolis and during their pregame interviews. A few of the Mason team members had never worn a suit, and it was refreshing to see them all looking like well-groomed athletes. Liz even helped them shop for the needed clothes and advised them on the best. In contrast, the Florida players arrived in shorts, tee shirts, and flip-flops. The differences were noted on many occasions by the press. Jim and Liz Larranaga had prepared the team for this event in every instance. Interviews were professional, and the Mason players were considered some of the most articulate and polite of the four teams.

Mason played well but was overwhelmed by a very talented Florida team. Florida went on to beat UCLA for the championship. Many sports pundits said that Mason played better against Florida than UCLA.

# Chapter 33: Helicopter Parent

2005 I served as the University Chief of Staff at George Mason University. The President's suite of offices was on the outside of the building and surrounded a large waiting area with chairs and couches. Administrative assistant desks were just outside the offices. The reason for understanding the layout will soon become obvious.

Late one afternoon, I was chairing a meeting in another building and walked into a scene I will never forget. Dr. Alan Merten, Mason's President, told a man that he could not and would not treat anyone the way he did and would either leave on his own or the University Police would escort him off campus. As the man was leaving, I walked in the door. Dr. Merten then told the man that if he came back, he must apologize to each of the administrative staff, and then he could talk to the Chief of Staff, me.

My executive assistant told me what had happened before I walked in. The man entered the President's suite with his son, a senior at Mason. He demanded that someone allow his son to register for a particular class because he had to have it to graduate, and no one was listening to him. When an administrative assistant suggested he talk to the Department Chair or the Dean, the man became irate and verbally abused the assistant. Dr. Merten heard the commotion, came out of his office, and told the man he could not and would not talk to any staff member that way. That is when I came into the scene.

Within an hour, the man and his student son returned, and the man apologized to each staff member, and they took a seat in the waiting area. I left my office, introduced myself, and invited them into my office. My office had a round table that I used to hold meetings. I told the father to sit at the table and put the son in a chair directly across from me. I began my conversation pointedly at the son by asking about his status and the problem with his class. As the son began to explain, his father attempted to interrupt. I turned to the father and said, "Your son and I are discussing the issue. It is his to resolve, not yours." The father's attempt to intervene again prompted me to say, "Your son and I will address this issue together. You may listen or not. You interrupt again, and I must ask both of you to leave."

The son and I then began an informative and disappointing dialogue. I first asked his status as a student and learned he was a second-semester senior. When I asked what the issue was with a class, he explained that he had failed to take a required math class in his freshman or sophomore year and could only graduate if he completed the class. He then explained that he was working and had limited time to take the class. According to the registrar's office, the class he wanted to take was full, and he needed help to add the class to his schedule. I then asked the following questions:

"Have you talked to the professor teaching the class?" Answer: "No."

"Have you talked to the Department Chair about the class?" Answer: "No."

"Have you made an appointment to talk with the Dean of the College about the class?" Answer: "No."

"So, you have made no effort to resolve the issue, and you believe it is now someone else's problem to solve?" I looked at the father and saw a look I can best describe as chagrin. It was apparent that the relationship between the father and the son required the parent to solve all the child's problems, with the child taking no responsibility. I was looking at a twenty-one-year-old man who would graduate in six months and enter the workforce, having never assumed responsibility for his actions.

I could have lectured the father on his responsibilities of raising a child, but it could not have been useful at this point. I instructed the son to start with the professor teaching the class, and if that did not succeed, go to the department and seek assistance. I later learned that the professor allowed the student to force add the class when he needed it.

Dr. Merten's actions that day did not go unnoticed by the staff across the university. How he had thrown out an abusive parent circulated quickly through the staff. It became one more reason those at George Mason loved and appreciated Dr. Merten.

I learned later that a survey had been completed within the last year that attempted to find out whom students were talking to as they went across campus. Not surprisingly, 50% answered that they were talking to a parent. When asked why they were talking to a parent, more than 50% answered that they had a problem and needed parental assistance. Helicopter parenting does not end in high school.

# Chapter 34: When Presidents Visit

Close proximity to Washington, DC, has many benefits and opportunities. For those studying politics and public policy, it is a rich field of research. Proximity also means that Members of Congress and Presidents will often find a reason to visit the campus of George Mason University.

In 2005, the White House called the George Mason President's office and scheduled a visit by President George W. Bush. The President turned the planning for the visit to me. I convened a group of staff and faculty to help me tackle the logistics and administrative requirements.

Two days before the visit, the Secret Service advance team visited campus, and we discussed the site visit, transportation, and security requirements. As the President was returning from Camp David, he would be arriving by helicopter, and we needed to identify an appropriate landing site for Marine One, the Presidential helicopter. Marine One is not a small helicopter; the only suitable landing zone was a lacrosse field adjacent to the Field House.

My landing zone experience with helicopters was limited to much smaller and lighter aircraft. We did not know and learned later that most athletic fields' soil is not compacted and, thus, is quite easily furrowed by heavy equipment.

The President's visit went off without a hitch. He arrived on time, gave his speech, and left on time. Later that day, an angry phone call from the women's lacrosse coach told me in no uncertain terms how the heavy helicopters had ruined the lacrosse field and that I was to blame. A short trip to the lacrosse field confirmed her concerns, and I found deep furrows across the field made by Marine One as it arrived and departed. The grounds crews had much work before the next women's lacrosse home game.

Early in his Presidency, Barack Obama visited George Mason to deliver what was later described as a policy announcement. As usual, I was tasked as the coordinator and met with the Secret Service to review the site, the transportation arrangements, and event security. All went well until shortly before President Obama arrived.

To set the scene, the concert hall where the speech would be delivered has a unique entry and access road. The road in front of the concert hall is one way leading across the front of the building. Access to the parking deck is available immediately past the concert hall. The parking deck can also be accessed from a street that ends at the parking deck with no street access to the front of the concert hall.

The head of the Secret Service detail and I were standing on the second floor of the concert looking out on the street that ran in front. We could see the road leading into the parking deck. We watched as a somewhat dilapidated pickup truck came down the parking deck access road and stopped. It then started to drive into the road in front of the concert hall, either ignoring or missing the one-way do not enter signs. Just as the pickup truck entered the one-way street the wrong way, three black-clad figures in body armor and carrying submachine guns leaped out of the shrubbery and stopped the pickup truck.

The Secret Service chief said, "Those are my guys, and they are supposed to stop anyone from entering from that direction." We watched as the driver was taken from the pickup, questioned, and then released to exit in the opposite direction.

After the President had departed, my assistant and I reflected on what had happened. We both agreed that somewhere there is someone out there telling everyone that when you are at George Mason, you better obey the traffic signs. We also felt sympathy for the individual who likely had no clue that the President of the United States was about to arrive and he had penetrated the security zone.

# Chapter 35: Grandfather Joys

Grandchildren bring joy to grandparents in many ways. I am privileged to have some wonderful grandchildren, three boys and two girls. Opportunities to spend time with them are often difficult to find. If I was still working and they were in school or involved in athletic activities, time was precious. Fortunately, I found a way to give us a week together in the summer. The Road Scholar program is an amazing organization offering exciting educational trips for individuals and families. One of their programs is for grandparents and grandchildren and is tailored to the grandchild's age. The stories are the four summer "adventures" I took with four of my grandchildren.

The offerings provided by Road Scholar vary both in type and location. For example, there are educational tours of major cities and more adventurous trips to national parks. In preparation for any of the four trips, I selected five or six "adventures" that our grandchild and I would both enjoy. I then allowed the grandchild to choose one of the five or six. Once they chose, it was time to book a flight and make the reservations with Road Scholar.

### *Aidan and the Grand Canyon*

Aidan Thomas O'Malley, our oldest grandson, was eleven in 2014 when he and I took the *Exploring the Grand Canyon and Beyond* Road Scholar program. We flew to Las Vegas and then a rental car to the outskirts of Sedona, Arizona, where the program was based. Before landing in Las Vegas, I told Aidan he would see many slot machines in the airport. He was still amazed at the number of slot machines and agreed they would take as much money as possible from those departing.

The trip was truly an adventure. We explored the largest and driest cave in the west and learned about the flora and fauna in the Grand Canyon and the Native American tribes that had lived there for thousands of years. The trip's highlight was rafting down the Colorado River and learning about the geological anomalies and historic efforts to learn about the Grand Canyon. This picture is Aidan enroute to our portage  point on the Colorado River. Spending such quality time with a great teenager was a real joy.

### *Sean Mount Rushmore and the Badlands*

Sean Michael O'Malley, Aidan's younger brother, and I made the next Grandchild/Grandparent adventure in 2015. Sean chose the trip to South Dakota, which included a visit to Mt Rushmore, the Badlands, horseback riding, riding down a mountain, and digging for fossils in one of the largest archeological sites in the region. If you visit Mt Rushmore alone, you will park about a

half mile from the entrance. Our bus dropped off at the entrance, and our guide had already obtained our entry tickets. This is one of the great advantages of Road Scholar programs. All entrance fees are included in your program, and there is little or nothing that you must do except enjoy the adventure. This picture show Sean riding down the mountain on the Alpine Slide. After the program was over and we had a few hours before heading back to the airport, I decided we might as well do our laundry and arrive home with only a few dirty clothes. Much to our daughter's surprise, Sean learned how to do laundry, fold his clothes and put them away. She remarked later that this was a great learning experience for Sean.

### *Hunter and Glacier National Park: Raft, Ride, and Slide*

In 2016, our youngest grandson, Hunter Thomas Jacks, and I flew to Missoula, Montana, on our Road Scholar summer adventure. We hiked Glacier National Park, rafted down the Flathead River, and traveled through the trees in an aerial adventure course. We stayed in the Hilton Garden Inn in Killaspell, and all the grandchildren enjoyed the indoor pool at the end of every day. The noise level in the pool was very high, and you could tell these 9, 10, and 11-year-olds were having a wonderful time. We went by chair lift to the top of one of the highest mountains and took a slide to the bottom. This picture

is our rafting adventure. Hunter and I are wearing white hats, me in front and him in the back. I cannot say enough good things about the Road Scholar program for grandparents and grandchildren.

### *Ellie and Chattanooga*

In August 2022, our youngest granddaughter, Ellie Rose Hennessey Jacks, chose the Road Scholar Trip: *Underwater and Outer Space*. Who would have thought that a city in the middle of Tennessee would offer so many great attractions? We rode a historical train across Chickamauga Creek and heard tales of notorious outlaws, Civil War soldiers, and Native American warriors. In the Mission Control Room, designed after the NASA Johnson Space Center, she flew a simulated space mission to the International Space Station and back. We toured The Challenger Center, built as a memorial to the astronauts lost on the Challenger Space Shuttle mission on January 28, 1986.

The opportunity to drive a Duck Boat on the Tennessee River was a highlight for Ellie. We also visited one of the only remaining carousels with hand-carved horses; the grandchildren could ride it before it opened to the public. The Chattanooga Aquarium is one of the best I have ever visited. The multiple levels provide access to the various species in each one of the separate areas.

The program's final and most spectacular part was the Rock City

and Ruby Falls visit. This picture is of Ellie and me in front of the tallest waterfall inside a cave. The changing light in the cavern gives an unworldly glow to the waterfall and the large pool beneath. Walking the trail on Rock City was informative and enjoyable.

The most touching moment of any of the four summer adventures was on our way home. Sitting in the plane shortly before landing, Ellie put her hand on my arm and said, "Papa, that was the greatest adventure I have ever had. Thank you." That's all it takes to warm a grandparent's heart.

# About the author

Dr. Hennessey served in the United States Army for over 28 years in successively responsible leadership positions and retired as a Colonel. During that time, he received multiple awards for distinguished service.

After retiring from the Army in 1993, Hennessey was appointed the University Chief of Staff at George Mason University. Until his retirement from the University in 2013, he remained a teaching faculty member and taught undergraduate and graduate-level public management, policy, and governance courses.

Since 2005, Dr. Hennessey has served as the founder and president of Hennessey Management Consulting, LLC, a consultancy with clients in the federal and state governments and the higher education community. He is an avid reader and writer. Dr. Hennessey and his wife Barbara, reside in Leesburg, Virginia. 

He has published three other books over the past year, ***Fairy Tales and War Stories, Out of Time in the Desert***, and ***Ghost Soldiers of Gandamak***

www.ingramcontent.com/pod-product-compliance
Lightning Source LLC
Chambersburg PA
CBHW040829010826
48978CB00012BB/673